FIREBALL

FIREBALL

JIMMY SANGSTER

ISBN: 1-7324226-8-0
ISBN 13: 978-1-7324226-8-1

Published by
Brash Books LLC
12120 State Line #253
Leawood, Kansas 66209
www.brash-books.com

PUBLISHER'S NOTE

This book, the previously unpublished fourth novel in the "James Reed" series, was written by Jimmy Sangster in the late 1980s and was recently discovered among his papers. We wish to thank Stephen Gallagher for his help unearthing the original, dot-matrix print-out from the archives at De Montfort University in Leicester, England and Denise Fields for retyping the manuscript.

ONE

The name of the tennis club should have been warning enough for James Reed to stay away: The West Malibu Tennis and Racquet Club. Nothing was west of Malibu except the Pacific Ocean. A flier had come through his mailbox advertising the new club and offering a discount to early sign-ups. James had been about to drop the flier in the trash along with the rest of his junk mail when he saw the note scribbled on the back:

"Hi, Mr. Reed, come pay us a visit. It's on the house."

It was signed by Paul Menzies.

He couldn't remember a Paul Menzies and he didn't play tennis any longer, he didn't know if someday one of his future tenants might want to join a local club. In fact, the couple from back east who were currently renting the main house had asked the other day about a tennis court. Maybe this would be more convenient than the old club further along the coast.

But then he decided the current renters were a miserable pair, always complaining about something. What did they expect for their $10,000-per-month?

But he kept the flier anyway. Anything that said "on the house" was worth looking into, even if it did usually turn out to cost double what it should.

A couple of weeks after receiving the flier, he had lunch in the San Fernando Valley with the man who had once expressed interest in being his literary agent until he had realized that James didn't know how to write. The reason for the lunch turned out to be that the agent had a script and he hoped that James might use his influence to get his movie star ex-wife Katherine to read it. If she liked it, the script immediately became a hot project.

James had the good sense to finish the lunch before telling the man that, not only did he not have contact with Katherine any longer, but even if he had, he wouldn't ask her any favors, either for himself or for anybody else.

Driving home after the meeting, he didn't feel as pissed off as he thought he would. The lunch had been good and it had gotten him away from the beach, something that happened less and less these days. In fact, he had a contented little buzz going as he drove back across Malibu Canyon. Then three miles before he reached Pacific Coast Highway, he spotted the sign announcing the West Malibu Tennis and Racquet Club.

On an impulse he turned off and followed the narrow track road through a valley in the hills until he reached what he assumed was the Club: four cement courts surrounding a small wood hut. The place looked like a deserted building site.

As he pulled up, a young man came out of the hut, looking towards him. He was wearing shorts and no shirt. It was the muscles that did it. As the man turned and went back into the hut, James remembered where he had last met Paul Menzies. In fact, he remembered him quite well. It was just the name he'd forgotten. Given the circumstances of their meeting, perhaps he'd never even known it. They'd met on the beach, around six weeks ago; a July 4th barbeque given by Harry and Beth Davis who lived a few houses up. Come one, come all, providing you brought your own bottle or, better still, two. Menzies had been one of the guests, or maybe he'd just come with one of the guests. James didn't remember.

What he did recall was that Menzies had remained sober while everybody else drank themselves legless, which was just as well because just before dark one of the female guests decided to go for a swim. Fifty yards out, she got a cramp and started to yell for help. Three of the male guests dove into the sea to rescue her. Two of them sunk like stones almost immediately, weighed down by the amount of booze they'd consumed. They staggered back to the shore throwing up vigorously. The other made it half-way to the distressed female before getting into trouble himself. It was left to Paul Menzies to save both of them from drowning.

As it that wasn't enough, later that evening a gang of over-sized kids from east LA came wandering along the beach looking for trouble. They found it when they tried to hassle the party. Paul Menzies proved that not only was he a polite young man with big muscles who could swim like a fish, he could also be a mean mouthed son of a bitch, who matched his words with actions.

He nearly broke the gang leader's arm and threatened to blind one of his cohorts with a barbecue fork if they all didn't "fuck off out of here 'n stop botherin' my friends." It had been touch-and-go until James, who had seen trouble coming a few minutes earlier, had walked out of Harry Davis's house nursing the shotgun that Harry kept mounted above his oar. He'd lined himself up beside Paul Menzies. This had been enough for the gang, who were looking for a good time rather than trouble. They shambled off, mouthing dire threats, heading down the beach to find another party they could gatecrash. James had returned the shotgun to its place behind Harry's bar, Paul Menzies had come into the house with him.

"How come you're the only one of that bunch out there who was gonna do something 'bout those creeps?" He had a faint drawl which placed him south of the Mason Dixon line.

"The others had more sense," said James.

"Shit, they'd have let those bums rape their wives 'n girl-friends and not lifted a finger."

"That they would."

Paul Menzies gave a snort of disgust, "I don't believe it"

"You must be new in town," said James.

He'd spent a few more minutes with Paul before rejoin-ing the party, during which time he discovered that the young man had been in LA for just over a month. He had come from Hendersonville, North Carolina and his ambition was to be rich and famous but while he was waiting he'd keep his body in shape, play a little tennis, work out, stuff like that y'all.

James had rejoined the revelries, gotten even drunker and not spoken to Paul again for the rest of the evening. He was on his way home along the beach around 11:00 p.m. when Paul Menzies fell into step beside him.

"You live on the beach Mr. Reed?"

Mr. Reed. James liked that. He pointed to the main house looming above them. His tenants, in keeping with their general deportment, were early-to-bedders, so the place was dark.

"That's me," he said.

"Wow! I suppose you don't happen to have a guest house for rent?"

"The guest house is where I live," said James.

"You're putting me on."

James assured him he wasn't. Because he quite liked the young man, he invited him through to the guest house for a non-alcoholic night cap. There was a moment's hesitation from Paul at the invitation.

"It okay," said James, "I'm not after your body."

He'd stayed for about half-an-hour, drinking a glass of Perrier to James's scotch. He told James he was staying with some friends further along the beach who had brought him to the party, and he was looking for a place of his own. He liked LA fine. He just knew he was going to make something of himself out here. And, no sir, he didn't care for another glass of Perrier, he'd be on his way now, thank you kindly for your hospitality. That had been the last James had seen or heard of him until now. All this he remembered as he walked towards the hut. He practically reached the door when Paul re-emerged, pulling on a shirt and apologizing for being caught half-naked.

"How you been Mr. Reed?" he asked as they reestablished identities.

"Fine. How about you?"

"Couldn't be better. Look it what I'm in charge of."

James looked. A wooden shack and four empty tennis courts. They were liable to stay that way too. Here in the fold of the hills, the temperature was at least fifteen degrees higher than it was out on Pacific Coast Highway.

"I sure got lucky," said Paul.

"You own the place?" asked James.

"Heck, no! This Texan, he owns it. I just manage it for him. You play tennis?"

"I used to."

"You wanna hit a ball?"

"It's too hot."

"Come to the clubhouse. I'll get you a cool drink."

James followed him into the wood hut. It was dark and just as hot inside. A large soft drink machine took up one wall. Paul lifted a front panel, fiddled with something and a can of Diet Coke clanked into the tray at the bottom. He threw it to James.

"On the house," he said. He threw a tennis bag off a beat-up old sofa and told James to sit a spell.

"I really ought to get going," said James.

"You only just got here. I gotta give a lesson in fifteen minutes but 'til then, I got nothing but time. I'll tell you 'bout the guy who owns this place. It'll give you a laugh."

So, because he felt a little sorry for Paul Menzies, James sat down and listened to the story about the guy from Texas whose name happened to be David Crocket.

"So help me, it's true." said Paul. "He carries a copy of this birth certificate around with him just to prove it. Okay, so he buys this little bitty canyon here and he's gonna build the purdiest residential development this side of Corpus Christy, which is where he comes from originally. But in Corpus Christy they

5

don't have no California Coastal Commission, and the real estate sales lady who sold him this here canyon didn't tell him, which was downright dishonest of her. On the other hand, from what I hear tell, she and him were making it pretty heavy at the time, so he probably got no more than what he deserved. Can you imagine makin' it with your own real estate lady!"

James could. In fact, real estate ladies were the number one category in his little black book. Real estate and interior decorating were the two professions most favored by newly divorced, and consequently available, Los Angeles ladies.

Paul fetched himself a drink from the machine as he continued with this story. It seemed that escrow duly closed on the deal and Mr. Crocket, who sounded to James just about as dumb as they come, moved in the bulldozers. He's taken the top off a fairly large area before he was told he was breaking the law. The whole deal went into litigation. It was going to be a long drag through the law courts. In the meantime, pity to have all that newly flattened land going to waist. Permission was asked for and granted for the laying of the tennis courts. Paul heard about the whole thing through the wife of one of the attorneys who were involved.

"A real nice little gal, 'cept she likes to screw around. That's how I met her. I was screwing her in the afternoons while her husband was down the office or court or wherever. Would you believe it! She never told me she had a husband. I make it a rule Mr. Reed, never to screw around with a married lady. I don't know what it's like here in California, but where I come from, you're liable to get gelded if you're messin' with another man's wife."

Paul followed up on the information and got the job of running the place. Maybe, when the litigation was finally done, the tennis courts would have to go, but until that time, if Paul had anything to do with it, the West Malibu Tennis and Racquet Club was going to thrive.

About then, there was the sound of a car arriving.

"That there'll be my lesson," said Paul.

James downed his coke and prepared to leave. As he stood up, Paul's lesson came into the hut. James decided right there and then he might take up tennis again.

"Mrs. McCoy, Mr. James Reed," Paul made the introduction.

Mrs. McCoy flashed a smile and stuck out her hand. "Are you the James Reed who used to be married to Katherine Long?"

James owned up to being the same James Reed.

"The movie star Katherine Long?" said Paul, impressed.

"This is quite a coincidence," Mrs. McCoy said. "I met your ex-wife last week. She told me about you."

Immediately James was on guard. Why would Katherine be talking about him? "How is she?" he asked, not particularly interested to know.

"Just fine," said Mrs. McCoy apparently satisfied to leave it there. She was about thirty-five years old, with a slim, hard body, a good face and a healthy head of blonde hair. Her skin was smooth and unblemished. Her eyes wide and blue, her mouth cheerful and her hand clasp dry and firm. Altogether, his favorite type of lady.

"I met your ex-wife once," said Paul, trying to stay in the conversation.

"I feel that was myself sometimes," said James, without taking his eyes off Mrs. McCoy. "Are you from around these parts?"

"New York."

"I was there once," said James.

"And?"

"Hated it."

"I guess that makes us quits," said Mrs. McCoy. "I feel the same way about Los Angeles."

"So do I," said James.

"We should get started with our lesson, Mrs. McCoy," Paul was definitely feeling left out.

"Maybe we could have a game sometime," said James.

"I'm only here for a few more days. Perhaps next trip. Nice to have met you, Mr. Reed." She walked out of the hut.

"Thanks for dropping by Mr. Reed," said Paul before following her out. "Come again. And tell your friends about us ... your ex-wife too, if she plays tennis. Even it she doesn't, maybe she'd autograph a picture to me. I'll hang it up behind the desk over there. Be good for business."

Before James could answer one way or other, Paul had gone.

As James walked to his car, Paul and Mrs. McCoy started to hit balls. She was a powerful hitter with a nice smooth action. She'd probably kill him in a game. Her car, a compact, was the only other in the lot, parked well clear of his battered old Corvette, as though to avoid contamination.

He climbed in and hit the starter with much anticipation. He'd run the battery flat so many times during the past months, it was a wonder it was able to hold a charge for longer than ten minutes. Maybe he'd have an excuse to hang around the tennis club until the Auto Club showed up. It would give him a chance to get to know Mrs. McCoy better. But, ever perverse, the car started first time, belching a lot of black smoke. He waved once towards the tennis players as he drove away. They didn't even see him. Maybe Paul Menzies and Mrs. McCoy had more going for them than tennis lessons. James doubted it. Hadn't Paul said he didn't screw around with married ladies? Mrs. McCoy sounded like a married lady, even if she didn't look much like one. Still, either way, it was none of his business.

He stopped at the market on the way home and bought himself something for his supper. As he climbed back into the car, he noticed the flier for the tennis club as on the front seat. He screwed it up and threw it away.

He managed to slip into the guest house without being spotted by his tenant, something he'd learned to do since he'd realized the tenant invariably had something he wanted to complain about.

Setting out for his jog on the beach, he wasn't so lucky. He was just letting himself out of the back gate when he heard his name called from the terrace.

"Mr. Reed….!" Landers was leaning over the rail nursing a large drink. James couldn't be sure, but he suspected that he'd been there most of the afternoon just waiting for this moment.

"What's the problem, Mr. Landers?"

"You wanna come up?"

"I'm going for a run."

"This won't take but a minute."

James opened the gate at the bottom of the steps and walked up to the terrace. Landers was wearing bathing shorts and a floppy, straw hat. James thought his sixty-five-year-old body looked like a melted candle. Landers and his wife came from New York. Rich and retired, for twenty years they'd been going to Florida for three months each year. This year, they had decided there were too many Cubans in Florida so they'd try California instead. They hadn't stopped complaining since the day they arrived.

As he came onto the terrace, James could see Mrs. Landers in the living room watching TV. She never seemed to do anything else. In fact, James hadn't seen her outside the house since the day they moved in two months ago. Landers didn't offer him a seat.

"How much rent am I paying you, Reed?" Having got him onto what he considered his own territory, Landers obviously felt he could dispense with the "Mr."

"Ten grand-a-month, Mr. Landers," said James. Every conversation with Landers started the same way.

"Right. Ten grand-a-month. That comes to three hundred and twenty-two dollars and fifty-eight cents per day, which is the amount I'm gonna hold back from the rent check for this month."

"Okay, Mr. Landers. Whatever you say," James started back toward the beach.

"Don't you want to know why?"

"I'm sure you have a good reason."

"Bet your ass I have. Carmelita tells me the washer and dryer ain't working." Carmelita was the maid they brought with them from New York. She was as old and bad tempered as her employers.

"I'll call the repair man right away," said James.

Landers was bored. He wanted an argument. He needed an argument. "They get their asses here today or I'll hold back another three hundred twenty-two dollars," he said.

"Don't forget the fifty-eight cents," said James.

There was a fair breeze blowing in from the sea. It kept the air clear and bright but it also created little whirlpools and eddies of sand. James was the only person on the beach, unusual for this time of year. After five minutes, he decided he wasn't enjoying his run so he cut it short. As he let himself back in through the rear gate, Landers called down to him from the terrace.

"You call that repair man right away or you're gonna regret it."

James ignored him.

The phone was ringing as he came into the guesthouse. He switched on his answering machine and monitored the call.

"This is Megan McCoy, Mr. Reed. We met at the tennis club this…"

James picked up the receiver, switching off the machine at the same time, "I'm here, Mrs. McCoy."

"I'm glad. I hate answering machines. I'm sorry to bother you, but I wonder if you and I could have a little talk."

"Certainly," said James.

"Paul told me you have a house on the beach which you sometimes rent."

"Yes, I do."

"I might be interested in renting it."

"Just you, or you and Mr. McCoy?"

"Just me. Can we discuss it?"

James told her he'd be more than happy to discuss it. What he didn't tell her was that he already had a tenant who had a lease for another month with the option to extend. "Maybe we could talk about it over some dinner this evening?"

There was a slight hesitation on the other end of the line. Finally, she told him she liked the idea of dinner. He could pick her up at seven thirty. Then she had second thoughts. "The car I saw at the tennis club. Is that your only means of transport?"

"Afraid so," said James.

"Maybe I'll meet you someplace. Where do you suggest?"

Quick calculation. How much was he prepared to invest in a dinner with Megan McCoy? Might as well go the full bundle. After all, she said she was interested in renting the house. That made the meal deductible. He suggested a restaurant in Santa Monica where he'd taken a date, the bill was well over two hundred dollars.

"I rather hoped I wouldn't have to drive down to the beach again."

"I thought you were staying at the beach,"

"I am staying in Beverly Hills."

"In that case, you choose the restaurant," said James, who hadn't dined in Beverly Hills for the past six months.

"Why don't you come to my hotel. We'll make up our minds over a drink," she suggested. "I'm staying at The Beverly Hillcrest."

James said he'd be there are seven thirty.

He dusted off his only decent jacket and pressed a pair of pants. He'd taken his good shirt to the laundry a couple weeks ago and not gotten around to picking it up yet, so he ironed one of his beach shirts. At six thirty, just as he was ready to leave the house, there was a knock on the font door and he opened it to Landers.

"Did you call the repair guy yet?"

"I did," lied James.

"When's he coming?"

"Tomorrow for sure," said James.

"See that he does," said Landers. "Or you'll blow another day's rent."

James came out of the guest house and closed the door behind him. "Tell me Mr. Landers, are you and your wife happy renting my house?"

"What's it to you?"

"I mean, if you want to leave, it's okay with me."

"There's another month to go on my lease." There was a trace of panic in his voice that James hadn't heard before.

"Maybe you'd be better off someplace else. Like San Diego."

"Don't get smart with me, Reed."

"I mean, for three hundred and twenty-two dollars and fifty-eight cents a day, you should be happy. Instead, all you do is bitch all the time."

Landers hesitated a moment before answering. "I'll give it to you straight," he said finally. "I like to bitch. It's all I got left nowadays."

Maybe James had misjudged him. "You'd have liked it better this afternoon if I'd given you an argument."

"I was banking on it," said Landers.

"Tomorrow I'll give you an argument," said James. "Right now, I've got a date."

"It figures," said Landers. "First time I see you looking like anything better than a beach bum."

James started towards the front gate. "If it makes you feel any better, I didn't call the repair man. I forgot."

"Boy, is that gonna cost you," said Landers.

"You try and stop one cent of the rent money and I'll instruct my attorneys to sue you."

"You try it, buddy. I got attorneys in New York that'll eat your attorneys alive."

"Yeah? Just let them try it," snarled James.

"Don't worry. You give me any trouble and they'll skin you alive."

James went out the gate.

"And don't you forget it, schmuck," Landers yelled after him. The panic had gone from his voice. It seemed all was right in his world once more. James was surprised he hadn't figured him earlier.

The Beverly Hillcrest is a fairly modest place, perched at the summit of Beverly Drive where it connected with Pico Boulevard. To the west was 20th Century Fox studios and across the road was the Hillcrest Country Club, founded by the Jewish community of Los Angeles when they were barred from joining the Los Angeles Country Club a couple miles away.

At various times, James had been a guest at both places. The Hillcrest was much better. He parked his car in the hotel lot and walked into the lobby. He asked at the front desk for Mrs. McCoy's room number. They weren't at liberty to give out room numbers, however they would announce to Mrs. McCoy that she had a visitor.

Five minutes later, Megan McCoy stepped out of the elevator. She was dressed neatly, without flamboyance, and without much style. She was made up carefully to look as though she wore no makeup at all and her hair was pulled from her face and tied with a ribbon at back. James was disappointed. It wasn't what he'd been expecting. The woman standing in front of him didn't exactly match the woman he'd met earlier his afternoon at the tennis club. Not as striking; certainly not as sexy. Maybe it was the tennis clothes that were responsible. They'd shown off her excellent figure, something the skirt and sweater she was wearing didn't do.

"How about a drink upstairs while we decide where we're going to have dinner?" she said.

"Your room?" asked James, mainly because he felt it was expected of him.

She smiled, "The bar. It's on the top floor."

James had been there before. It wasn't particularly attractive but it had a pleasant view out across the roof top of Beverly Hills.

There was a group of Japanese having a noisy dinner in the far corner of the restaurant, but the bar was empty. James ordered a scotch; she ordered a white wine spritzer. While they waited for their drinks, she commented on the view and he started to wonder what the hell he as doing there.

"Tell me about your house," she said, finally.

"First you tell me something," said James. "How come if you're staying here, you go all the way down to Malibu for a tennis lesson?"

"We knew Paul from way back," she said.

"We?"

"My husband and I."

"Your husband's not with you on this trip."

A fractional pause, "No, he's not."

Something was going on here, thought James, without much interest. "Where is he? Back in New York?"

"He travels."

"But not to Los Angeles."

"Not this trip, Mr. Reed. I can't go on calling you Mr. Reed. Which is it, James, Jimmy, Jim?

"James."

"Tell me about your house on the beach, James."

He'd already decided it was too expensive for her. Visitors who stayed at the Beverly Hillcrest and rented compact cars couldn't afford ten grand-a-month rentals. But he'd gone to some trouble pressing his pants and his shirt, and he didn't want the evening to finish before it had started, even if the Megan McCoy sitting across the table from him wasn't the same woman he'd gotten the instant hots for this afternoon. He began to describe the house. He'd hardly started when she interrupted.

"I'd like to see it," she said.

"Any time," said James.

"How about right now."

"Right now, I'm hungry, and I don't think my tenants would like the idea."

"You did not tell me it was already rented."

"They're on a month-to-month."

"But I'd need it right away."

James shrugged. "Sorry. But let's have dinner anyway."

"Really, you could have told me!" There was a sudden edge to her voice that grated on James. He wondered what he'd ever seen in Mrs. McCoy.

"People who rent ten grand a month houses are usually prepared to wait a couple weeks for the privilege."

Her wide blue eyes opened even wider. "Ten thousand-a-month! Paul told me it was a tiny little place. A guesthouse."

"That's where I live. I rent out the main house. Paul knows that."

"I must have misunderstood, I'm sorry."

"Don't worry about it," said James. "Are we still on for dinner?"

He didn't much care one way or the other.

"I'd like dinner very much."

"Where would you like to go?"

"You choose."

That suited James fine. He suggested The Palm. Sure, it would cost a lot of money, but at least the food was reliable and, as far as he knew, he still had a charge account there, a legacy of the days when he had been married to Katherine.

"Shouldn't you make a reservation?"

"I'll do it from the lobby," said James.

She went to fetch her car while James called The Palm from the pay phone in the lobby. They had a table for two available in ten minutes. He hung up and went outside. There was no car in the forecourt. He looked out across the dark parking lot. A couple of dozen cars, none of them looking as if there were about to go anyplace. No headlights. No engine sounds. No Megan McCoy. At that moment, a parking valet came sauntering around the corner and saw James.

"You want your car, mister?"

"What happened to the lady?" James asked.

"I didn't see no lady."

"She just came out. Three minutes ago."

"I've been taking a leak. Sorry."

James looked around the parking lot again. Still no sign of movement.

"You want me to look for her?" asked the parking valet.

"Forget it," said James. He headed out into the parking lot, wondering if he'd recognize her car from this afternoon. He recognized it. It was parked on the far side of the lot, with an empty space either side of it. At first, James didn't see Megan. The door on the driver's side was open. He looked in the car. Nothing. He straightened up again and looked around. Then he heard a whimper, not unlike the sound one would hear from a puppy in pain. It came from under the car and it wasn't a puppy. It was Megan McCoy.

She looked like she'd been beaten quite badly. She had either been rolled under the car or she had scrambled there for her own protection. Before dragging her out, James instinctively walked around the car once. Whoever was responsible could still be lurking in the vicinity. He didn't see anybody. Only then did he go down on his knees and gently ease her out from beneath the car.

She was a mess. Her face was covered in blood, her blouse was ripped and that too, was blood stained. Her knees were badly grazed and she'd lost one of her shoes. As he helped her to her feet, he could see that most of the blood was due to a nosebleed. She wasn't in quite as bad a shape as he'd first imagined. She slumped against him, he put an arm around her. She had stopped whimpering. Now she started to say something. He stopped her.

"Don't try to talk yet, I'll get you back inside and call the police," he said.

"No police," she said. At least that's what it sounded like.

"Spit out the blood," he suggested.

She did. This time he heard her loud and clear, "No police."

"Suit yourself," said James, who wasn't about to argue with a bleeding woman in a parking lot. "Come on, I'll help you to your room."

She shook her head vigorously. Some blood splashed across James's only jacket. "Can't … go back to hotel."

"Why can't you go back to the hotel?"

"He'll come here."

"Listen. Whoever did this is probably long gone by now."

"Please. Not the hotel." She was looking up at him now. She'd taken a hefty smack in the eye. Already it had started to color and swell. But she wasn't being hysterical. She was deadly serious. "He knows I'm here. He'll try again."

He realized she wasn't talking about any old neighborhood mugger or rapist. "Who are we talking about?" he asked.

There was a fractional pause before she answered, "My husband."

That was all James needed right now. To get mixed up in a domestic fracas. As a cop in London, a hundred years ago, he and his colleagues would rather have faced a hopped-up, ax-wielding maniac than get involved in a domestic battle. It was impossible to adjudicate and there was no winning side. "If you don't want to go back to your hotel, where do you want to go?" he asked.

"I don't know," she said.

It was difficult to tell through the blood and the mess, but James believed she had started to cry. "How about another hotel?" he asked.

She shook her head, "He'd find me."

James wanted her to stop shaking her head. Every time she did, she splashed blood. His jacket was going to have to go to the cleaners. "Take my word for it. The police would be best."

"No." The tone of her voice was adamant.

"How about I take you to Paul Menzies. He's an old friend, you said"

"I can't involve Paul," she said. Then she looked up at him. He knew what was coming before she opened her mouth. Sure, you can't involve old friend Paul Menzies, but new schmuck James Reed is an entirely different matter. He thought of a dozen reasons why he should say no.

"May I come and stay at your place?" she asked.

"Why not," he said.

James talked her into returning to the hotel if only to tidy herself and pick up the things she might need. She insisted he come in with her. Upstairs, she made him go into the room first to check it out. When he announced it was all clear, she came in and bolted the door behind them. She disappeared into the bathroom. James heard running water. He'd had a good look at the damage to her face on the way up in the elevator. One black eye, a cut lip and a bloody nose. Not exactly life-threatening injuries. Maybe he could talk her out of coming down to the beach.

"Maybe this isn't such a good idea," he called out.

She appeared in the bathroom door. She'd removed her torn blouse and her skirt. She was wearing brief panties and she had a small towel clutched to her breasts. She looked extremely vulnerable and sexy.

"I'm sorry. What did you say?" she asked.

"I said maybe it isn't a good idea you coming home with me."

"There's nowhere else …" she said, her expression starting to crumble.

"I think it would be best if you stayed here. Tell the desk you don't want any calls or visitors. Have them change your room if it'll make you feel better."

"The only thing that'll make me feel better is getting out of here." She started to cry in earnest now. She used the small towel she was holding to wipe her eyes, which meant it wasn't covering her breasts. She took longer over this maneuver than was strictly necessary. James tried to avoid looking at her breasts and failed dismally.

"Suit yourself," he said.

She stopped wiping her eyes and asked James to hand her a sweater and a pair of pants which she took back into the bathroom. She reappeared a couple of minutes later announcing she was nearly ready. She threw some things into a small overnight bag. Most of her stuff she left where it was. Just as they were about to leave, the phone rang. She jumped like somebody had let off a firecracker in the room, but she made no attempt to pick it up.

"Aren't you going to answer it?" James asked.

She shook her head. "Let's go."

Downstairs, she handed over her key at the desk and the two of them walked out. The parking valet James had seen earlier was still on duty. He went to fetch her car. As they stood waiting for him to return, she moved closer to James and tucked her arm into his. She looked around nervously, searching into the dark corners of the parking lot. Finally, the valet drove up in her car.

"You left it unlocked, lady," he said, as he climbed out.

"You drive," she said to James.

As he pulled out of the parking lot, he wondered briefly when and how he would pickup his own car, then he decided the hell with it. Maybe he would get lucky and somebody would steal it.

He turned right on Pico Boulevard and drove as far as the San Diego Freeway. Already he had started to regret what he'd let himself in for. There was something a little flaky about Megan McCoy. He had a serious conviction that the fucking he might get, and it was by no means guaranteed, wasn't going to be worth the fucking he'd be getting.

For a moment he couldn't make up his mind which route to take to Pacific Coast highway, freeway or surface streets. It was this indecision that confirmed his earlier doubts. They were being followed. He started to swing onto the freeway, then he changed his mind and pulled back onto Pico. The car immediately behind him nearly drove into the freeway sign as the driver corrected his direction to follow them.

James didn't say anything to Megan right away. Only when they reached Santa Monica and drove down onto Pacific Cost Highway heading North, did he bring it up, and then only peripherally. He didn't want to scare her.

"What does your husband want?"

"Me," she said.

"Badly?"

"He lost his temper is all, I'd rather not discuss it, if you don't mind."

"Suit yourself," said James. "I was just curious to know how far he'd it's having your back that he wants."

"How do you mean?"

"Will he get violent?"

"You saw what he did to me."

"I mean gun violent. Knife violent."

"Why?"

"Because I think he's following us. Somebody's following us."

Instinctively she looked back over her shoulder. There were half a dozen cars back there, anonymous behind their driving lights.

"Are you sure?" she said.

"I'm sure."

She looked back again. "I don't know how you can tell."

"I'll show you," said James.

He made a signal and pulled into the side of the road. There he stopped. The car following them started to brake, then the driver changed his mind and drove past them, pulling up fifty feet further on. Either their pursuer was very bad at what he was doing or he didn't mind it being known that he was following them.

"Convinced?" asked James.

"Not really."

James opened the door and started to get out.

"What are you doing?" she said quickly.

"If you don't believe me, maybe you'll believe him. I'll drag him on over."

She looked horrified at the idea. "No … don't do that."

James had no intention of doing any such thing, and after a suitable pause, he allowed himself to be coaxed back into the car.

"Your husband?"

"It could be a private detective. He's used one before."

"But it was your husband who beat up on you back at the hotel."

"I told you it was." A slight edge creeping into her voice.

"What does he do, this husband of yours?"

"What do you mean?"

"I mean, does he hire this private detective to keep tabs on you so he can drive on over from time-to-time and knock you about."

"There's no need to get sarcastic."

James turned in the seat so he was facing her. "Mrs. McCoy, I don't know what the hell is going on, and I don't much care. What I do care about is being made a fool of, which I think you're doing right now."

"You think I made these bruises up?"

"No. Someone took a poke at you. You tell me it was your husband, okay. I accept that. But you won't go to the police. Then you tell me you're being followed by someone who might be your husband but who also might be a private detective who he employs occasionally. But you don't want me to call him on it."

She started to say something, but he wasn't even listening.

"You've got the real hots to come back to my place tonight and you flashed your girlish charms a couple of times just to make sure I'd get the message."

"Now you're being offensive," she said.

"From where I'm sitting, all this adds up to trouble, Mrs. McCoy. But it's your trouble, not mine. And I aim for it to stay that way."

He restarted the car, flashed his lights once at the car parked in front of them, just in case the guy had gone to sleep on the job, then he pulled back onto the highway and made a U-turn, heading back towards the Santa Monica Freeway.

"What are you doing? Megan wanted to know.

"Taking you back to your hotel."

"You can't. He might be waiting for me."

"Call the police."

"He's my husband, for Christ's sake."

"So, divorce him," said James.

He dropped her back at the Beverly Hillcrest twenty minutes later. Once she understood that his mind was made up, she stopped trying to change it. She sat stiff and tight lipped for the last few miles. Five minutes before they reached the hotel, she reached into the back of the car for her overnight bag. She unzipped it and took out a brown manila envelope which she transferred to the car glove compartment, then she zipped up the bag again. As soon as he pulled up at the front of the hotel, she got out of the car.

"I'll leave the keys with the valet," he called after her.

She ignored him, walking into the hotel without a backward glance.

James parked her car next to where he'd parked his earlier. As he climbed into his Corvette, he saw the car that had been following them move into a parking slot on the far side of the lot. The lights went off, but nobody got out.

Maybe he'd go chat him up…find out what kind of crazy broad he'd nearly gotten involved with. On the other hand, maybe he wouldn't. Whoever was sitting in that car might be a minor crazy. There were a lot of them around these days, guys who'd just as soon shoot you, or stick you with a knife, as pass the time of day. Perhaps she'd been wrong and it was her husband and he'd seen James, and now assumed the two of them were upstairs about to get it on. Any moment now, he'd get out of the car and go upstairs and murder the both of them. Still nobody got out of the car.

The hell with it, thought James. He turned the key in the ignition. The engine emitted a tired whine of protest before giving up the ghost entirely. He turned the key again. Nothing happened. Not a murmur.

Great. So now he was stuck. Except he still had the keys to Megan's car. He could either drive it home and bring it back in the morning or he could use it right now to jump start his own.

The jumper cables were no problem. As far as his car was concerned, they were as essential a piece of equipment as the brakes or the steering wheel. Without worrying if the guy on the far side of the lot was watching him or not, he fetched the jumper cables from the trunk, opened up the hood of Megan's car and connected the two batteries. Still his own car wouldn't start. Finally, he disconnected the cables, locked his own car, and went to the hotel lobby where he asked the desk to call Megan's room. After a couple of minutes, the desk clerk announced there was no answer.

Obviously, she still wasn't answering the phone. He asked for some writing paper and an envelope.

"My car won't start, I've borrowed yours. I'll have it back by 9:00 a.m."

He signed it James Reed, stuck it in the envelope and asked the night clerk to have it delivered to Mrs. McCoy's room.

When he went back outside, the other car had gone. The watcher, whoever he was, had obviously got tired of watching. He climbed into Megan's car and started the motor. Then he remembered the envelope she'd put in the glove compartment. He opened the compartment and took it out. It was a plain manila envelope and it felt like it held some papers or a notebook. Maybe she'd need it tomorrow before he could get her car back to her. Then he decided, the hell with her for the second time that evening. He dropped the envelope on the seat beside him and headed for the beach.

He was more than half way home when he realized he was starving. It was nine thirty, and he hadn't eaten yet. On Pacific Coast Highway, he pulled into the first place that didn't look like it was going to cost a fortune. He ordered himself a steak, a salad and a bottle of house white. He'd long ago learned that if you were drinking cheap wine, it was better to stick with white.

"That's a small bottle. Right?" said the waiter, a pretty thirty-year-old guy, who couldn't take his eyes off a couple of surfers sitting at a table across from James.

"A regular sized bottle," said James.

"There's two of you then."

"Just me," said James.

The waiter took his eyes off the surfers for the first time. "A whole bottle, all for yourself. My goodness."

He brought the bottle to the table and opened it without bothering to show James the label.

"Is it dry?" asked James.

"Sure, it's dry," said the waiter. "Dry as a bone."

The wine was sweet, the steak was overcooked and the salad was limp. James complained to the hostess on the way out.

She shrugged. "What do you want? The chef is off Tuesdays."

James reminded her today was Wednesday, but she'd already lost interest. He drove the rest of the way home, put the car in the garage next to the Landers' rented Cadillac and went to bed. Just before he slid over the edge into sleep, the events of the day drifted across is consciousness. They left no impression at all.

TWO

The day started like any other. A glass of orange juice, a run on the beach, a quick look up and down the street on the off chance somebody might not have taken in their newspaper, then a shower and cup of coffee … by which time he was ready for anything. Except, as with most days over the past couple of months, there was nothing for him to be ready for.

Sure, he had to call the repair man for the washer and dryer in the main house and no doubt, Mr. Landers would come up with something else to bitch about before too long, but neither event was going to fill his day. He could start painting the guest house, something he'd been putting off for a month now, or he could get out the extension ladder and climb onto the roof of the main house and check out a leak he'd fixed a couple months back, which he suspected might spring again. The pilings supporting the terrace on the beach side of the main house needed some minor repairs before the end of summer, and the terrace itself needed a fresh coat of paint. On the other hand, he could have Landers move his car and he could clean out the garage, something he'd been meaning to do since Christmas. That's when he remembered yesterday evening and the fact he still had Megan McCoy's car. It was just after ten. He was surprised she hadn't called.

He looked up the number of the Beverly Hillcrest. When he got through, he asked to speak to Mrs. McCoy. It seems she still wasn't answering her phone. Would he care to leave a message?

"This is James Reed. Tell her I'll have the car back by 11:00." Next he called the Auto Club and arranged for them meet him in the hotel parking lot at 11:00.

As he was letting himself out of the guest house, Landers was coming from the main house. "What time is the repair man coming?"

James went back inside and called the repair shop with Landers standing over his shoulder. The girl on the line said they'd be at the house between noon and four p.m., providing she could reach them on the radio.

He must have been out already this morning. His rented Cadillac was parked so close to Megan's compact in the double garage that James had to open the passenger door to get in. As he did so, Landers appeared at the garage door.

"Hey Reed!" James turned toward him. "What happens if they can't contact the repair men? What happens then?"

"Then I guess your washing stays dirty and you save yourself another $322.58."

Landers grinned wolfishly, "Bet your ass," he said.

James slid across into the driver's seat, backed out of the garage and pointed the car toward Beverly Hills.

At the Beverly Hillcrest, he turned the car over to the parking valet. The Auto Club hadn't yet put in an appearance. He went into the lobby and asked the desk clerk to put him through to Mrs. McCoy's room. There was still no answer. Either she'd gone out while nobody was looking or she was still just not answering her phone. He told the desk clerk that he'd brought her car back and that the keys were with the valet. Then he went out to do battle with the representative of the Auto Club, who had just shown up. He was a tidy looking black guy with slicked down hair, rimless glasses and clean white coveralls. He'd come from a Beverly Hills garage where he was accustomed to dealing with badly behaved Mercedes or recalcitrant Rolls Royces. A car like James's was beyond his experience. After checking and double-checking James's Auto Club card, he walked around the Corvette a couple of times without getting any closer than three feet.

"Holy shit," he said. "I don't know where to begin."

"I'm not asking you to fix it," said James, "I just want her started."

"Listen, man. I'll do you a big favor. Give me five hundred bucks and the pink slip and I'll tow it someplace."

"Where?"

"What do you care. Out of your life man."

"It's a classic," said James.

"A classic pile of shit. Have you ever serviced this car? You know, changed the oil, brake fluid, taken it for a wash, that the kind of thing?"

James ignored the question, which answered it. "Just start her up."

"I'm not going anywhere near that heap of junk. I'd likely catch AIDs or something."

"You're a funny man," said James. "Here's twenty. Now start her up and get the hell out of here."

The guy folded the twenty neatly and stuck it in his coverall pocket. He went to fetch jumper cables from his truck.

"I already tried jump starting her," said James. "Last night."

"Look, man. This is Beverly Hills. Round these parts, they bend a fender, they junk the car. I'll give it to you straight, if it ain't a tired battery, forget, I can't help."

The car started first time, belching out a noxious cloud of black smoke. The guy looked moderately pleased with himself. He packed away his jumper cables and stood shaking his head sadly as James signed his work order sheet.

"Listen, mister. You get another problem, do me a favor, call someone else." He climbed into his truck and started the engine. Just before he drove off, he hit the horn. "Hey mister!"

James walked over to see what he wanted. The man leaned out of the cab.

"Here, man, I gotta figure you need this more than me." He handed James back his twenty-dollar bill.

Sometime while this was going on, a patrol car belonging to the Beverly Hills Police department had pulled up under the front portico. Both officers had gone into the hotel. Now, as James stated to climb into his car, he saw the desk clerk come to the door of the hotel with a uniformed cop and look out across the parking lot. James climbed into the driver's seat, slammed the door and, because there were cops in the vicinity, started to buckle up. He was about to back out of the parking slot when the cop he had just seen with the desk clerk banged smartly on the window. James wound it down.

"You wanna kill the motor, sir?" said the cop. He was a young guy who managed to look aggressive even though he hadn't yet lost his acne.

"No, I don't want to kill the motor," said James. "It might not start again."

"Kill the fucking motor, buddy," said the cop.

James revved the engine hard, trying to build up a small charge in the battery before he switched off. The cop didn't read it that way and James suddenly found himself peering down the barrel of the cop's .38.

"You're dead meat before you're out of the lot," said the cop.

Fuck the battery, thought James. He killed the motor.

"Now get out of the car." The cop had backed off a couple of paces, his gun held two handed. Not only was he young, he didn't look too sure of himself, so James got out very carefully. "Hands on the roof, spread your legs."

James did exactly as he was told, slowly and carefully. The cop now called to his partner, who had appeared at the door to the hotel, "Charley! Get over here."

Charley was older, a grizzled veteran of twenty-seven or eight.

"What you got here, Spike?"

"Guy's been using the broad's car. When I prodded him, he tried to make a run."

"Is that right?" Charley said to James, who was still standing with his legs apart, his hands on the roof of the car.

"No," said James.

"Got some kind of ID?" asked Charley.

James started to go for his billfold. "Hold it, fella!" said Spike, who still had his gun on James.

"Hip pocket," said James.

Charley dipped into James's hip pocket and extracted his billfold. From it he produced his driver's license. He looked at it, front and back.

"Okay Mr. Reed. Maybe you can help us out with a couple of things. How come you tried to make a run?"

"I didn't. I revved the motor is all."

"Sure. Just when I told you to kill it," said Spike.

James started to explain about the battery then he decided the hell with it. "Can I straighten up?"

Charley patted him down quickly and efficiently, "Sure you can."

James stood up straight and turned around. Spike was still holding his gun on him.

"You wanna put that away?" said James.

"Not until we get some answers," said Spike.

"Answers to what?"

"The desk clerk just told us you delivered Mrs. McCoy's car," said Charles. "What are you, a mechanic? Someone who works for a car rental company?"

"Neither," said James. "I'm a friend who borrowed her car last night. I suppose you're gonna tell me she reported it stolen." James had known she was pissed off last night, but not *that* pissed off.

"Why would she do a thing like that?" Charley asked. He sounded genuinely interested.

"The lieutenant's here," said Spike.

They all looked towards the front of the hotel. An unmarked car had just pulled up. A large untidy looking man, about fifty years old, stepped out of the car. He could see what was happening in the parking lot. It if made may impression on him, he didn't show it. He said something to his driver and lumbered over.

"He's a mean sumbitch," said Charley to nobody in particular.

"Go tell him about this joker we got here," said Spike.

Charley thought about it for a moment before deciding it wasn't a bad idea and met him halfway. Spike straightened himself in the presence of a superior, but kept his gun trained.

James watched as Charley spoke quietly to the big guy who nodded a couple of times, his eyes flicking once towards James.

Finally, the lieutenant nodded again. "Okay, I'll take it from here." He looked toward Spike. "Put your gun away, son," he said. Spike did so reluctantly. The big man moved over to James.

"Hi there, Mr. Reed. You don't remember me, do you?"

"Nope," said James.

"Micklehaus, Richard C."

He was even larger close up, a great bear of a man with thinning hair that he combed sideways across his pink scalp in an unsuccessful attempt to hide this baldness. His nose proclaimed he was a drinking man.

"I'm sorry," said James. "I still don't remember."

"I spent a coupla nights sleeping over at your ex-wife's house when she was getting those crazy letters. You and me played some chess."

Now James remembered him. "You beat my ass."

"I sure did," said Micklehaus.

"You were a lot thinner."

Michlehaus shrugged. "A lot of things have changed since then." He was looking at James's car. "You used to drive a Rolls."

"It belonged to my wife."

"Can't win'em all. How you been?"

"Okay, up to now. What's going on here, anyway?"

"The boys didn't tell you?"

"All the boys told me was to get out of the car and spread my legs."

"Yeah, well, they haven't had as much experience as you and me."

James had forgotten. Micklehaus knew about his background. They'd swapped cop stories while they were waiting for a maniac writer of threatening letters to carry out his threat to break into the house and do a Ted Manson on Katherine and whoever else he found.

Micklehaus continued. "As far as I can tell, and I only just got here, we've got ourselves a grade 'A' homicide. Least, that's how it sounds to me."

"Mrs. McCoy," said James with dreadful certainty.

"That's what they tell me. You knew her?"

"I met her. Last night. What happened?"

Micklehaus explained that a chamber maid had let herself into Megan's room and discovered the body at about the same time James returned McCoy's car. "You wanna see the body?"

He didn't, but Micklehaus persisted. "Come on! It'll be like the old days for you."

"I wasn't on homicide."

"Come see the body, Mr. Reed, I insist."

James caught a certain tone in his voice. "Really insist?" he asked.

"Yeah." He threw an arm around James's shoulder and started to propel him towards the main entrance of the hotel. He had no way out. "Got your keys?" he asked.

"They're in the car," said James.

They passed Spike, who had put away his gun. "You wanna get Mr. Reed's car keys for him, son?"

"Yes sir," said Spike, nearly saluting.

"Just check he ain't left nothing of value in the car first," said Micklehaus.

"Don't cars require search warrants?" asked James.

"Sure they do, Mr. Reed," said Micklehaus. "But who's searching? C'mon now. Let's go visit the *corpus delicti*."

"I'd still prefer not," said James, wanting now to see just how far Micklehaus was prepared to go.

"You don't want to see the body. Okay, you're entitled? So, I'll tell you what we'll do. You can wait for me down here in the hotel lobby. We'll just slip a pair of cuffs on you in case you get bored waiting and decide you wanna go home before I'm through upstairs."

"So, let's go see the body," said James.

Whoever had killed Megan McCoy had been looking for something. The room had been turned inside out. Megan herself was on the bathroom floor, her head propped against the show door. She was wearing the same clothes James had last seen her in.

"How did she die?" James asked.

"Somebody strangled her with her tights." Micklehaus said and turned to talk to a couple of plainclothes forensic techs who'd just arrived in the bedroom.

James looked at her. The bathroom stank of shit and death. His stomach started to curl. He walked back into the bedroom and joined Micklehaus. "Okay, I've seen the body. Can I go now?"

"Talk first, Mr. Reed."

"What am I supposed to talk about?"

"Tell me what you and she did last night — what time you picked her up, where you went, what time you brought her home, why you were driving her car and why you knocked her around. That'll do for starters."

For the first time, James started to feel he might be in trouble. "Do I need my lawyer?"

"Not if you come up with the right answers."

"Can we go someplace else?"

"What's the matter Mr. Reed, the stink of death getting to you?"

"You're a grade 'A' bastard, lieutenant," said James.

Micklehaus grinnned. His teeth weren't very good. "Ain't that the truth," he said.

Micklehaus had commandeered a room across the hall. He evicted a couple of cops and closed the door and he was alone with James. "Okay, Mr. Reed. So, tell me."

"You tell me something first. How did you know Mrs. McCoy was beat up last night?"

"The desk clerk. He said you were the one who did it. You arrived to pick her up. You had a drink upstairs. You went out to the parking lot and you came back in two minutes later with her all beat up and bloody. The two of you went upstairs together."

"Then he went off duty."

"How'd you know?"

"If he hadn't, he'd have seen us go out again five minutes later and her come back on her own half-an-hour after that. For that bit of information, you can check with the night clerk. Now can I go?"

If Micklehaus was disappointed, he didn't show it. "You seem to have all the answers, Mr. Reed. Suppose you tell me how it was from your side of the fence. From the top."

James told him. Micklehaus let him finish without interruption.

Only then did he start to pick holes. "How come you didn't call the police when you found her under the car?"

"She wouldn't let me."

"You didn't try to talk her into it?"

"I figured it was her business."

"So you decided to take her home instead. Were you gonna hump her, Mr. Reed?"

"We'll never know, will we lieutenant?"

"Guess we won't. So, there you were, driving this broad down to your pad on the beach when you decide you're being tailed. She says maybe it's her old man, then again maybe it's some shamus he rents from time-to-time. About then, your pecker starts to wilt, so you turn right round and bring her back here to her hotel. Am I right so far?"

"Correct," said James, deciding to ignore the embellishments.

"You drop her off, then find your car won't start, so you take hers."

"I borrowed hers. I left her a note."

"We haven't found any note."

"Maybe you haven't looked. I left it with the night clerk."

"I'll check it out. Anything else you want to tell me?"

"Whoever was tailing us followed us back here. When I went out after leaving the note, he'd gone."

"I suppose it would be too much for you to remember what kind of car he was driving."

James shrugged. "A midsize coupe, dark."

"Is that it?"

Micklehaus shook his head. "Man. And you used to be a cop."

"It was a long time ago."

Micklehaus picked up the phone and dialed the front desk. He asked the duty clerk to look for a note addressed to Mrs. McCoy that should have been delivered last night. The clerk came back on the line almost immediately, Micklehaus nodded a couple of times before hanging up.

"The note was in her mail slot. Looks like you weren't shitting me, Mr. Reed."

"Disappointed, lieutenant?"

"Can't win 'em all." He wandered over to the window and peered out across Pico Boulevard to the lush greenery of the Hillcrest Country Club. "Any ideas?" he said, without turning around.

"Find the husband?"

"We're already looking."

"And the shamus."

"For him, too."

"Check to see if there's anything missing from her room."

Micklehaus turned back into the room. "You're not being much help, Mr. Reed."

"Tough," said James. "Can I go now?"

"Sure. Leave your address with one of my people." James headed for the door. "And don't leave town."

There was a cop in the passage outside of Megan's room. The door was half open. Two or three others had arrived during the past few minutes. James could see them milling around inside the room. He left his address and went down to the lobby where a small group of guests were gathered chattering among themselves. They were beginning to wallow in the vicarious thrill of just being here. He could imagine the conversation:

"Sure, we had a good time in LA. We went to Disneyland, the Universal Tour and we had a murder right in our own hotel. That's real value for your tourist dollar!"

❧ ❧ ❧

Spike and Charley were leaning up against their car talking to three girls on roller skates. The girls wore their hair in braids and their shirts outside their shorts. They were all chewing gum and pretending to be impressed by whatever Spike was telling them.

"You got my keys?" James asked.

Spike hardly looked at him. "On the front seat."

James headed across the lot towards his car. Spike called after him, "I see you on the road in that heap and I'm gonna bust you for littering the highway." His audience giggle appreciatively.

Megan's car was still where James had left it. He remembered the envelope he'd left on the front seat last night. He didn't recall noticing it on the drive up this morning. It had probably slipped between the seats. Maybe he should tell Micklehaus about it. Then he decided, fuck him. He's such a hotshot cop, let him find it for himself. He climbed into his own car. It started first time. As he pulled out of the parking lot, the first of the local TV news crews were arriving in their station wagon. If you could believe what you read in the papers, especially the out-of-town ones, murder was not big thing. One occurred in Los Angles every fifteen minutes. But this one had all the ingredients of a media event: An attractive woman, in a Beverly Hills hotel, was strangled with her own tights after going on a date with James Reed, ex-husband of superstar Katherine Long.

Right now, he'd slid out from under the eagle eye of the media. Hopefully Spike and Charley wouldn't make the connection and Micklehaus was too professional to bandy his name around without something to back it up. There was no doubt that the media would eventually get wind of his involvement but hopefully, by then some of the hysteria might have died down.

The guilts didn't start to get to him until he was halfway home. He tried pushing them to the back of his mind, but they spilled out again. So he decided okay, let's drag'em out and deal with them.

Megan had known she was in danger. That's why she'd begged him to take her back to his place on the beach. If he hadn't been so pig headed and insisted on taking her back to the hotel, she'd still be alive. On the other hand, whoever killed her might have tried it anyway .... down at the beach. In which case, he could be dead too. That made him feel a little better. But not much. Whichever way the sliced it, she'd made an appeal for help and he'd turned her down.

"I'm a shit," he decided.

It was hardly a fresh bit of self-analysis. He'd been aware of it for a long time, positively reveled in it on occasions. Let's hope that Micklehaus was a good enough cop not only to run the husband to ground, he thought, but also to come up with enough evidence to make the murder charge stick. Maybe he should have told the police about Paul Menzies. After all, Paul was the guy who had introduced them and Paul had known both Megan and her husband from way back. Shit ... he might even know where the husband was right now. He should talk to Paul right away, have him contact Micklehaus.

Instead of turning off Pacific Coast Highway down to the beach road, he continued up the hill past Pepperdine University and hung a right on Malibu Canyon. Five minutes later, he was turning off into the West Malibu Tennis and Racquet Club. There were two cars in the lot. Four nubile young girls were playing a ragged game of doubles on one of the courts, the other three were empty. Paul was wearing just a pair of tennis shorts and was leaning against the hut, watching the game and calling out a lot of advice.

"Move your feet! Watch the ball! Bend your knees! Racquet up! Racquet down!"

It made no difference. The game was a shambles. It looked like none of the girls had ever been near a tennis court before.

They were around sixteen years old, dressed in shorts and bikini tops. They were all trying to impress Paul with their bodies since they could hardly do it with their tennis. Paul saw James arrive and came to meet him. "Hi, Mr. Reed! Come for a tennis lesson?"

James's arrival had caused a temporary slow down of the game. The girls were all looking towards him, sizing him up.

"Looks like you got your hands full," he said.

"Baby bimbos," said Paul, not unkindly and without bothering whether or not the girls could hear him. They did, but it didn't seem to worry any of them. Obviously, what they saw in James failed to impress because they returned to their game.

"You wanna a cold drink of something?" Paul asked.

"Just a couple of words," said James.

"Come on inside the clubhouse, it's cooler."

James followed Paul into the wooden hut. It wasn't any cooler unless one leaned up against the drinks machine, which packed its own refrigeration unit.

"You heard from the police yet?"

"Don't tell me. They're gonna close this place down. Shit, man, just when—"

"Hang on," said James, interrupting. "I'm talking about Mrs. McCoy."

"What about her?" Obviously, he hadn't heard from the police.

James told him and watched him crumple. Paul did everything but burst into tears. His big, muscled body seemed to shrink as he collapsed into the only chair in the place. He buried this face in the hands for a long time. James kept quiet. He was fascinated. So much grief. Obviously, he and Megan had been closer than he'd realized.

"Sorry to be the one to bring you the bad news," he said.

Paul shook his head without removing his hands from his face. He mumbled something unintelligible.

Beginning to feel a little embarrassed, James stepped outside the hut, just as the four girls were coming off the court. There was only a narrow walkway between the court and the hut. James was suddenly being jostled by half-naked young bodies slippery with a sheen of sweat, smelling like ripe strawberries.

"Excuse me sir."

"Pardon us."

They slithered past him and into the hut, leaving him feeling breathless and very old. There was a low mumble of voices, finally punctuated by Paul's "Fuck off!"

A moment later they re-emerged. They glared their hate at James as they headed toward the parking lot. Everything had been cool before he'd shown up. They climbed into the two cars and drove off showering gravel over James's car. He waited a couple more minutes before going back into the hut. When he did, Paul was helping himself to a drink from the machine.

"You want something, Mr. Reed?"

"Give me a club soda," said James, who didn't want anything.

Paul punched the machine again and handed James his club soda.

"Son of a bitch!" he said.

"Yeah," said James.

"I mean, man ... son of a goddamn bitch!"

"That's how I felt," said James.

"She was a nice lady. A real nice lady. Son of a goddamn, fucking bitch."

"Right," said James.

Paul took a long swallow of his drink. "Son of a bitch," he said for the last time.

Now he looked towards James. "How come you found out so quick, Mr. Reed. It's been on the news or something?"

James told him.

"You and her had a date ... is that what you're saying?" said Paul.

"Hardly a date. She wanted to talk to me about renting my house. You told her about it."

"That's right, I did."

"Then my car wouldn't start. I borrowed hers to drive home. When I took it back this morning, the cops were already there. Listen, I came to tell you so's our can get in touch with the police."

"Why would I want to do that?"

"They're looking for her husband. Maye you know where he is."

"New York."

"He's in Los Angeles. At least he was last night."

"They reckon he croaked her?"

"It's likely. He knocked her around earlier in the evening."

James told him about the beating.

"She said her husband did it?" said Paul. He sounded doubtful.

"That's what she said," said James. "The name of the cop in charge is Micklehaus. Give him a call."

"Did you tell him about me yet?"

"No."

"Listen, Mr. Reed, I'd consider it a real favor if you didn't mention my name … to the cops I mean. It's not like I can help them or anything and who needs all that hassle. Say you met her on the beach. Its easy to meet folk on the beach. Happens all the time."

"You got a problem with the law, Paul?"

He looked slightly embarrassed, "Nothing heavy."

"How heavy? Traffic violation heavy?"

"This chick … she told me she was seventeen."

"One of the bunch who just left?"

"No, but it could have been. I mean … they're all the same. Shit, Mr. Reed, what is it about California that makes all the young chicks so hot to trot all the time? I mean … I gotta fight'em off. You live here, for Christ's sake. You know how it is."

I should be so lucky, thought James. "Sure, I know how it is," he said. "When did they get you for it?"

"A couple of months ago. When I first came out here. They said I committed statutory rape."

"Did you?"

"Rape her? Hell no. It was the other way around. Lucky for me the judge was a young guy. He took one look at this chick in the dock and he knew, man, he knew."

"What did you get?"

"Probation. So, like I wanna keep a low profile. Getting messed up with the law right now ain't gonna help any. You understand?"

"I understand. I won't mentioned your name to the police," James said "Tell me about the husband."

"What's to tell? He and Mrs. McCoy split up a couple of years back."

"You knew them both."

"Back east. They owned a house at Spring Lake … that's in New Jersey. My folks live there. The McCoy's were neighbors. They used to come down from the City most weekends in the summer. They had their own tennis court and they let me and some of my friends use it during the week when they weren't around. It got so I'd kinda just keep an eye on the place when they weren't there … they were nice people … at least, she was."

"What about him?"

"He was all right too, I guess."

"What does he do?"

"He's a politician of some kind in New York City. You sure it was him who beat up on her?

"That's what she told me. Why?"

"I knew them when they split up a couple of years back. Seemed to me, at the time, the whole thing was real friendly … a couple of nice people agreeing they didn't get along so good no more. No kids, plenty money, so let's just call it a day. That's how

I read it. Weird he should show after a couple of years and beat up on her."

James agreed it was weird. He finished his soda, warm by now. Paul walked out to his car with him.

"Where's your car?" James asked him.

"I don't have one. Can't afford it."

"So how do you get to and from work?"

"I walk. It's only four miles to the place where I'm shacking right now."

"Everyone has a car in California," said James.

Paul looked at James's car. He grinned. "So, when you gonna get yours, Mr. Reed?"

Nobody likes a smart ass, thought James, driving home. But he liked Paul. He felt sorry for him too. Out here just a few days and the poor schmuck gets hooked into a statutory rape charge over a girl who quite likely lost her virginity before she'd had her braces removed. So, he'd keep quiet about Paul and Megan McCoy. If Micklehaus ever got around to asking him how he'd met Megan he'd tell him, he'd say it was on the beach, like Paul suggested. Meantime, he'd keep a low profile and keep his fingers crossed that Micklehaus located McCoy and locked up the case before it became too much of a cause *celebre.*

James tried to figure the timetable. Husband wants wife back. Wife doesn't want to know. Husband flies out from New York to persuade her otherwise. She still doesn't want to know. He loses his temper and knocks her around in the parking lot. Then he gets scared at what he's done and splits. Changes his mind and calls her at the hotel to apologize. When she doesn't answer the phone, he comes over to apologize in person or perhaps lean on her some more. He sees her leaving the hotel with a strange guy carrying an overnight bag. Flip out time. Follows them. She obviously changes her mind and asks to be taken back to her hotel where the strange guy drops her off. Husband goes up to her room. No, she's not going to come back to him. One thing leads to another, tempers are lost, and he strangles her. It felt awfully convoluted, but sometimes life was like that.

The garage doors were open. Landers hadn't bothered closing them after James had left in Megan's car a few hours ago. James thought about trying to squeeze into the space that was left, then he decided the hell with it, he'd get Landers to move his car over where it belonged. He parked outside and, because he didn't want Landers to accuse him of being a sloppy landlord, he started to shut the garage doors.

"Mr. Reed?"

He'd been vaguely aware of a car parked across the street. He'd even registered subconsciously the fact there were a couple of guys sitting the front. Only now they weren't sitting in the car any longer, they were standing behind him. As he turned to face them, some long forgotten instinct surfaced at the back of his mind, an instinct possessed by all good cops and, apparently by ex-cops as well … the ability to sense a villain, not by how he looked or what he was wearing or even by what he said, but just by *knowing*. The two men confronting him were neatly dressed in jeans, tee shirts and casual jackets. They were clean shaven, short haired, around twenty-two or three years old. They were both large young men, their jackets doing nothing to hide the muscular development of their upper bodies. They looked like they'd been pressed out of the same mold, except one was dark and one was fair. They could have been anything form body builders to health food salesmen. James know without a shadow of a doubt that they were villains of a particularly nasty kind.

"Who wants to know?" he said.

"My name is Bill. This is Gary," said the fair one.

"Hi fellas," said James.

"You are Reed, aren't you?" asked Bill.

If he'd thought he could have gotten away with it, James would have denied it. But these guys were to cool and too smooth and too dangerous to mess with.

"I'm Reed," he admitted.

"We'd like a word," said Bill.

"Sure," said James.

Gary said something James didn't catch. "What did you say?" he asked.

"We don't want to talk in the street." His voice was flatter than Bill's and very soft.

"The street is fine with me," said James. "And whatever it is you're selling, I don't need any."

They weren't impressed. "Inside," said Bill.

"I'd prefer out here."

"Inside," Gary, this time.

Enough is enough, thought James. "Go fuck yourself," he said.

The two guys didn't throw up their hands in horror. They didn't swear back. They didn't even look at one another.

"Break his arm," said Gary.

A piece of iron pipe appeared suddenly in Bill's hand. At the same time, Gary grabbed James's arm, one hand just above the elbow, the other around the wrist. He gripped like steel clamps. He stepped clear, holding James's arm at exactly the angle Bill needed to break it with the iron pipe. There were no "tell us what we want or we'll ..." type threats. Both men knew exactly what they were doing and right now they were going to break his arm. They had moved very fast, James moved even faster.

"Why don't you guys come inside," he said.

✤ ✤ ✤

They wanted to know where the manila envelope had gone to. They knew that Megan had it with her when she left the hotel with James last night. They knew because as soon as James and she left, they searched her room and it wasn't there. She didn't have it with her when James dropped her back at the hotel some half hour later because they were waiting for her and they searched her personally.

"I saw the good job you did of it," said James.

"What's that suppose to mean?" said Gary.

"I was there, this morning."

"So?"

"The cops allowed me to view the body."

"What body? What are you going on about?"

Bill reached forward and tapped James lightly on the cheekbone with his iron pipe. James thought he'd broken his face.

"Gary asked what body you're talking about. Tell him."

"Megan McCoy's body," said James. If they wanted to play innocent, James wasn't going to argue about it … not while Bill was still holding his section of iron pipe.

Gary and Bill looked at each other. Then they looked back at James.

"We didn't croak her," said Gary.

"We just searched her," said Bill.

James knew they were telling the truth. There'd be no point in their lying.

"How'd she get it?" Gary wanted to know.

"She was strangled."

"You figure he knows?" Gary asked Bill.

Bill shrugged. "What difference does it make. We're here to pick up the envelope."

"Right," said Gary.

"I don't have it," said James.

They didn't believe him. Now if James would just turn it over to them, they'd not break his arm. If he didn't, not only would hey break his arm, but they'd break his leg, too. James didn't doubt them for one moment.

"The law's got it," he said.

This threw them slightly, long enough for Bill to start waving his lead pipe in James's direction. Before they could do him physical damage James told them about Megan putting the envelope in the glove compartment, and him subsequently forgetting about it until after he'd left the hotel.

"What's the chance the law won't have searched the car yet?" Gary asked.

"No chance," said James.

Gary told Bill to make a phone call. He dialed a number. James knew by the number of buttons he hit on the phone that it was a different area code. Bill didn't even identify himself to whoever answered the phone.

"Reed says the lady was croaked," he said. He listened a moment then looked towards Bill. "He already knows," he said. Then back to the phone. "No. He says he hasn't got it. He says she left it in her car and the law will have got their hands on it by now."

He listened for a couple of seconds, glancing once towards James, then back to the phone. "I don't know if he's telling the truth or not." Another pause for listening. "Okay. Will do." He hung up without another word.

"We gotta make sure he's telling the truth," said Gary.

"So, let's do it," said Gary. He produced a knife as efficiently as Bill had his iron pipe. One moment, empty hand, the next, lethal weapon.

"For Christ's sake," said James. "Call the cops. They'll tell you."

"You'll tell us," said Gary.

"I already did." It was no good. The situation was becoming Kafkaesque. They were going to torture him to extract the information he'd already given them. Since they wouldn't accept handle the truth, he'd have to try a lie. "Okay," he said. "I lied."

They didn't seem too perturbed. "So where is it?" asked Gary.

"In the bedroom."

"Get it."

James started towards the bedroom. Gary nodded for Bill of the iron pipe to go with him. He stayed in the living room confident enough to fold his knife away.

Still with no idea what he was going to do, James walked into the bedroom and over to the closet. The carryall bag, in which he kept his shotgun, was on the floor at the back. He couldn't be dead sure, but he thought, the last time he looked, there were a couple of loose shells at the bottom of the bag. There were certainly none in the gun. But it was all whistling the wind. There could have been a fully loaded Kalashnikov in the bag, there was no way he was going to get it out and into use with Bill and his lead piece standing right behind him. So, he reached onto the top shelf of the closet and groped behind the pile of dirty washing for the piece of equipment he once used when he was into exercising. A one-handed barbell used to develop the muscles of the arm. It weighted about seven pounds. He figured that if the was quick, he might be able to bash Bill's brains out before Bill reciprocated. It might have worked, except the barbell wasn't where it was supposed to be and he was just groping around in a pile of dirty laundry. He wondered briefly how much damage he could do it he hit Bill with a pair of undershorts. It was that thought that made him realize he'd started to panic. Okay, hot shot, calm down. But not too far down because you've got less than a second to come up with a bright idea.

What he came up with was a key. It was on the closet shelf, under the pile of washing. He had no idea what key it was or what lock it fitted. All he knew was it gave him a few more seconds. He pulled the key out and held it up for Bill to see.

"Key," he said, feeling like an idiot.

Bill nodded. He was nobody's fool. He could tell it was a key. James turned from the closet and walked past the bed to the built-in dresser. He tried to take quick mental inventory of what was in each drawer; surely there was something he could use as a weapon. Wishful thinking, he realized. He knew there was nothing. So, he did the next best thing and used the drawer itself.

When James had first moved to the beach, all the fitted furnishings in the guest house had been made of trendy stripped pine. After six months he'd realized that the sea air warped the wood so much that it could take a crow bar to open a drawer. So, he'd had the wood taken out and replaced it with metal that slid open easily on a steel runner. He reached for the top drawer, pulling it open, as Bill was moving up behind him. He just went on pulling, at the same time pivoting around. The drawer came clear of the dresser, swung in a short arc and caught Bill on the side of the head. At the same time, James lost his balance and tripped over the corner of the bed. The metal edge of the drawer sliced off Bill's ear as neatly as a surgeon's scalpel. It was the sight of his ear lying on the bed that got to Bill more than anything else. He stood for a long moment looking down at it, complete disbelief on his face. Then his hand went to the side of his head to confirm what he still couldn't quite comprehend. By that time, James had pulled himself together and regained his equilibrium. He swung the drawer again, flat into Bill's face. This time, he managed to get his full weight behind it. It knocked Bill backwards, clear off his feet. He landed on his back, out cold, his face a squashed and bloody mess. James didn't wait to assess the damage. He jumped across the bed and scooped up Bill's iron pipe from where it had fallen and moved to the side of the door just as Gary came in from the living room, knife first.

James broke his wrist noisily. But Gary was a pro, he wasn't going to let a little old thing like a broken wrist affect his work. With one arm dangling uselessly, he used the other to haul back and hit James so hard he practically went through the wall. If Gary had followed up the blow with another, everything would have been over. Instead he decided to kick James's nuts through the top of his head. He lashed out with his left foot. James saw it coming and managed to slide sideways so Gary's foot caught him on the fleshy part of this backside. It hurt like hell. James didn't like to think what it would have been like had the kick been on target. And because Gary with a broken arm was still a considerable threat, James used the iron pipe and broke his leg as well. He collapsed beside Bill, who was quietly bleeding all over the bedroom floor.

James went into the living room and poured himself a brandy. He drank it and poured another. He took the glass and went back to the bedroom to survey the damage while he drank it. Gary had dragged himself across the floor so that his back was propped against the bed. He was trying to straight out his broken leg with his one good arm. He was making a good job of it. Bill was still bleeding profusely from what had once been a reasonably well put-together face. If he didn't regain consciousness soon, he was going to choke to death on this own blood. James stepped into the room and putting his foot under his body he turned him so he was on this side bleeding all over the carpet instead of himself. As James came in, Gary stopped trying to sort out his broken leg.

"You want a brandy?" asked James.

"You're a dead man," said Gary.

"Does that mean yes or no?"

"Give me a brandy."

James fetched him a brandy. Bill had started to stir, so before going further, James fetched some twine from the kitchen and tied his hands behind his back. Then he dragged him to the sitting position beside Gary. He fetched his shotgun from the closet. He'd been right, there were two shells at the bottom of the bag. He loaded them both. Then he fetched a straight back chair from the kitchen and placed it in the bedroom doorway so that it was facing the two guys. He topped up his brandy and sat down for a chat.

It took Bill a good five minutes to fully recover. During that time, James was forced to untie his hands and retie them in front. That way Bill was able to mop at the blood which was still streaming from his shattered nose and from the hole where his ear had one been, using up every towel both clean and soiled that James could lay his hands on.

"You guys ready to start talking to me?" James asked.

"Go fuck yourself," said Gary.

Bill tried to say something similar. All he managed was gurgle and a spray of blood.

James felt he'd used up his entire supply of adrenalin for the next five years, the third brandy was making his head ache, he could feel the lump on his cheekbone where Bill had poked him with the iron pipe and he was going to have to refurbish his bedroom from the carpet up. He was extremely pissed off.

"Have you got any words of comfort for me before I slice off your other ear?" he asked Bill.

He was coming across like a real tough guy. He wasn't sure how long he was going to be able to keep it up. Bill mumbled something unintelligible. Then he spat out a mouthful of blood and tried again. "Go fuck yourself," he said.

Tough was not going to work with these guys. Just call Micklehaus and turn them over. So what if they didn't kill Megan McCoy? They sure knew a hell of a lot about her. And what had all this shit got to do with him anyway? Why should he bust his ass?

He went into the living room and called the Beverly Hills Police Department where he asked to speak with Lieutenant Micklehaus. The Lieutenant was out, the operator said. Was there a message?

"Can he be paged?" James asked.

It seemed that he could be if the call was important enough.

"Tell him James Reed needs to get in touch urgently," said James.

"How urgent is urgent?"

"Tell him I've got him a couple of material witnesses in the Megan McCoy killing."

The operator promised to have Micklehaus call James within five minutes.

He looked back into the bedroom. The two guys hadn't moved. Bill's bleeding had stopped. He was surrounded by every towel James owned, all ruined. Gary had regained consciousness and was trying to adjust the position of his leg again. The bedroom was a complete shambles, uninhabitable. Shit, how he had the gotten into all this? All he'd wanted was to do was jump Megan McCoy's bones. Now she was dead, he'd nearly been arrested as the prime suspect, he'd been bashed with an iron pipe and his house had been wrecked.

Gary had been talking urgently to Bill. As James came in, he stopped. Now the two of them just stared at James, flatly and with dreadful malice. Hopefully Micklehaus would be able to find a good reason to lock them both away. But, unless their names were already on the blotter, it wasn't likely. He might be able to hold them for a few hours as material witnesses, but any halfway decent attorney would have them sprung almost before the key turned on them. In which case, James was going to have to move houses, preferably to another country.

On the other hand, they were professionals. If whoever hired them would call them off, they'd go their way and not give James a second thought, in spite of what he'd done to them. Their injuries were an occupational hazard, only to be held against the perpetrator if the was still on their list of uncompleted business. So ... either Micklehaus would have to lock them up, or James would have to find out who they worked for and convince him that he'd told the truth about the envelope, which wasn't going to be difficult if Micklehaus had already found it.

But Micklehaus hadn't found it. He called fifteen minutes later. During that fifteen minutes, James sat looking at the two guys while they looked back at him, nothing was said by either side. The only time James tried to make some kind of conversation he was told first that he was a dead man and second, to go fuck himself. The phone call came as a welcome relief. James picked it up in the living room, glad to have the two guys out of his sight for a moment or two.

"Micklehaus. What do you want?"

"Did you search her car?"

"What's it to you? I got a message you got me a witness."

"I've got you two. Did you search the car?"

"Sure, we searched the car."

"What did you find?"

"What was I supposed to find?"

Micklehaus wasn't bright enough to play games over the phone. Obviously, he'd found nothing. Which meant that someone had gotten to the car between the time that James dropped it off at the hotel and when the police searched it. That meant they'd been waiting at the hotel for the car to show up. Probably been there all night, ever since they murdered Megan.

"What about these witnesses you say you got?" said Micklehaus, interrupting James's line of thought.

"They're here."

"Where's here?"

"My place."

"What are they doin' there?"

"Bleeding on my carpet."

"Is that right," he sounded mildly interested. "I'll send a car for them."

James gave him the address. "Better make that an ambulance," he added.

There was silence from the other end. "You're some kind of a tough guy, Mr. Reed?" It was a question.

"No lieutenant, I'm just your average kind of a guy trying to get on in this city without being hassled."

"Who's hassling you?"

"If you find out, perhaps you'll tell me," said James.

"Half an hour," said Micklehaus. He hung up.

James walked back into the bedroom to break the news. Gary was using his good hand to untie Bill's wrists. Given a couple of hours he might have made it. James thought about separating them, moving Bill into the living room. But he was still bleeding and James didn't want to have to replace the carpet in there as well as in the bedroom. He sat down in the chair again and looked at the two guys.

"The law's coming to collect you," he said.

They didn't say a word. In fact, they ignored him altogether.

"They didn't find what you were looking for," said James.

A glint of interest.

"The way I figure it, that means whoever killed the lady has got the goods. Would either of you like to report that to whoever's paying you? That way you can get off my back."

Still no response, but they were definitely interested. They needed one more push to get them over the edge.

"I'll make you a deal with you," said James. "Get on the phone and break the news. Then, if your boss can convince me he'll get off my back, I'll let you out of here before the law arrives."

"Deal," said Gary.

Bill looked as though he might say something, but he changed his mind. Instead he spat another gob of blood onto the carpet. James fetched the phone and Gary had Bill punch out the number while he held the instrument with this his good hand. It was answered almost immediately.

"He ain't got it," he said.

He listened for a moment. "No, they ain't got it neither."

Another pause. "Sure, I believe him."

Another pause. "How the fuck should I know? Maybe whoever croaked her got it. Maybe she stashed it someplace. Maybe she never had it in the first place."

Now he glanced up at James. "No, we didn't hurt him too bad. No, we don't have to croak him. What does he know, for Christ's sake? Okay. Listen, I think I broke my leg and maybe my arm. I might have to stay out here a few days. Sure. Bye." He hung up. "You're off the hook," he said to James.

"You've got ten minutes," said James. "Don't go to UCLA Medical Center, they'll take one look at the two of you and holler for the police."

"We're not stupid," said Bill.

You could have fooled me, thought James, but he didn't say so. Bill held his hands out in front of him for James to untie. Keeping a good hold on his shotgun, James cut the bonds with Gary's knife. Then he backed away and watched as Bill climbed to his feet, bent down and hefted Gary up across his shoulder in a classic fireman's lift. At least he'd stopped bleeding.

"You wanna get the doors for me," he said to James.

James preceded them out to their car, where Gary was lowered into the back, his leg stretched out along the seat. It said a lot for his constitution that he hadn't uttered a sound. Bill climbed in behind the wheel.

"What are you gonna tell the law when they show?" he said.

"What do you care?" said James. Bill started the motor.

"Wait a minute," said James, starting back towards the house. He reappeared a few seconds later and handed Bill something wrapped in a tissue.

"What is it?" he said.

"Your ear," said James.

It was a good question of Bill's. What was he going to tell the law when they arrived to collect their material witnesses? He was worrying about it as he came bank in through the front gate. Landers was coming from the main house.

"Jesus H. Christ," said Landers. "What happened to your face? And what you are carrying that gun for? Shit, you've got blood all over you!" He started to back away.

"What do you want Mr. Landers?"

"Nothing. Nothing at all. I'll talk to you later." And he was gone, no doubt to tell his wife all about the *meshuga* landlord. James went straight to the mirror over the bar and took the first good look at himself since all this had started. He had a livid bruise high on his cheekbone, where Bill had tapped him with the pipe, and lots of blood. Okay, so he didn't have to worry any longer what he was going to tell the law.

"One of them hit me with a lead pipe," he said to Micklehaus who was yelling at him on the phone.

The police ambulance had arrived, along with a patrol car. James had explained to the cops that the guys they'd come to collect had escaped not five minutes ago and, sorry, but he didn't know what kind of car they were driving and he only had a vague description of what they looked like. The cops had contacted Micklehaus on their radio, and he had called James right away.

"I should have done that myself," said Micklehaus. "Okay ... so who were they, these two material witnesses of yours?"

"They were looking for something that Mrs. McCoy was supposed to have had." James told him about the envelope, everything about it. He was heavily into the truth right now. He wanted to out of the whole messy affair.

"Is that what I was supposed to find in the car?" asked Micklehaus.

"That's where it was," said James.

"Where, exactly?"

"In the front seat. Maybe down the side. I don't know."

"It wasn't there."

"You already told me, Lieutenant."

"So, where'd it get to?"

"You're the detective," said James.

"Fuck off," said Micklehaus. He hung up. Thirty seconds later the phone rang again. "Don't you leave town," said Micklehaus before handing up.

James spent the afternoon taking up the bedroom carpet which he threw out along with most of the sheets and towels. He drove into Santa Monica to the shopping mart where he bought new linens, then he went to a carpet store, where he chose some new carpet and arranged for them to come measure and lay it. All in all, he was going to be out around $2000.

It was around five thirty when he got home. He hadn't eaten all day and the bruise on his face was beginning to feel as bad as it looked, which was pretty terrible. He poured himself a large scotch, debated whether or not to add water, decided to add another scotch instead. He took a shower, drying himself on one of his brand new towels. There was nothing that halfway tempted him in the fridge or freezer. He was going to have to go to the market or to a restaurant. Seeing he'd already spent two grand today, another $50 wasn't going to make any difference, so he went to Sally's Diner, a place that had just opened a mile or two along the coast, where the proprietors were still trying to build up their clientele so they were polite to the customers and served portions of food that halfway matched the prices they charged. Soon it would become popular and all that would change. James had been there once before, just after they'd opened. The gay guy who ran the place welcomed him like he ate there every night of the week. And because he was an old and valued customer, he was asked about his poor face at the same time as he was given a drink on the house because he must still be in considerable pain, "poor love."

Two hours and a bottle of wine later, James staggered out into the night, located his car and managed to drive home without slaughtering anybody on the highway. Landers was waiting for him. At least, James assumed he'd been waiting because as he was letting himself into the guest house Landers came out of the main house and called his name.

"Tomorrow, Mr. Landers," said James.

But Landers wasn't to be put off so easily. He came across to join James who was having trouble fitting the key in his front door.

"Are you all right?" Landers wanted to know.

"I'm fine," said James.

"It's just that earlier … last time I saw you … you looked terrible. Like you'd been in a fight or something."

James felt a rush of affection towards Landers, a sure sign he was drunker than even he had believed. "Okay Mr. Landers, what's your complaint this time? If I can take care of it, I will. If I can't … tough shit!"

"No complaints," said Landers. "At least, I got complaints that'll curl your hair, but that's not what I wanted to see you about."

"You wanna drink?" said James, finally getting the front door open.

"I wanted to give you this," said Landers. It must have fallen out of that car you borrowed. It was on the garage floor."

He handed James the manila envelope.

James came in and over to the bar. He put the envelope on the bar and poured himself a drink. He went to the bathroom. When he came back, the envelope was still there. He walked around it a couple of times. As long as he was behind the bar, he poured himself another drink. He picked the envelope up and hefted it, trying to guess what it might hold. A notebook, he decided, or a diary, or a paperback novel or half a magazine or just a bunch of paper. There was no writing on the envelope and it was sealed with transparent tape at both ends. No way was he going to get a look at the contents without tearing it open. On the other hand, maybe he didn't want to get a look at the contents. It was probable that Megan McCoy had been killed on account of what was in the envelope. Two heavy cats had been prepared to beat the shit out of him on account of what was in the envelope. "No, we don't have to croak him," Gary had said, referring to James, also on account of the envelope. Someplace out there was the guy who had employed Bill and Gary on account of what was in the envelope. Maybe it was a good time for it to just disappear. That way, perhaps nobody else would get killed or beat up or threatened on account of what was in the envelope. That's it, decided James. The envelope and contents are going to disappear, the envelope unopened, the contents unread. But one more drink first.

He had three more drinks. Then he carefully hid the envelope before staggering off to bed, too drunk to bother that there was no carpet in the bedroom and hadn't yet unwrapped his new bed linen.

THREE

There was somebody banging the Judgement Day drum. At least that's how it sounded to James as he groped his way out of sleep. He rolled over and looked at the bedside clock. It was eight thirty, he felt terrible and somebody was beating the shit out of his front door. Maybe, if he pretended to be as dead as he felt, they'd go away. They didn't, which probably meant it was Landers wanting to complain about the freezer of the dishwasher or the vacuum cleaner. So, fuck him, decided James. He rolled over and tried to dive back into the hole from which he'd just emerged. It didn't work. The banging persisted. After a couple of minutes, James climbed out of bed and, stark naked, went to put a flea in Lander's ear.

The girl standing outside his front door was around twenty-two or three years old. She was five foot, three inches tall and looked as it she might weigh around eighty pounds soaking wet. If she was disturbed at the sight of James answering the front door without any clothes on, she didn't show it.

"Mr. Reed?"

James, half closed the door and stuck his head round the edge.

"What?" He wasn't in the mood for small talk right now.

"You are James Reed, aren't you?"

"No," said James. He closed the door and started back towards the bedroom. Immediately, the knocking started again. He fetched his robe from the bathroom and went to answer the door again. "Whatever it is, I don't want it," he said. She was a very pretty girl, he decided. A little under-nourished for his taste, but cute nevertheless.

"I'd like to talk to you, Mr. Reed," she said.

"What about?"

"My name is Patsy McCoy."

"I'll tell you what Patsy. Why don't you come back later? Say around noon. Then you can say your piece and either I'll buy what your selling or I won't. But at least by then I'll be halfway civil." He started to close the door again.

"Megan McCoy was my mother."

"Ah," said James. Even one more reason to close the door firmly in her face. He stood back, "Come in," he said. "But not a word until I tell you it's okay."

He squeezed some orange juice and put on some coffee. She sat tidily on the sofa, watching him carefully. He drank the orange juice, trying to convince himself that it made him feel a little better and sat across from her.

"I am sorry about your mother," he said.

"She wasn't my real mother. She was married to my father."

"I'm sorry about your stepmother."

"I'm not. Well, I am … I mean … nobody wishes another person dead. But I didn't like her."

The coffee pot gurgled noisily from the kitchen. James stood up.

"Coffee?"

"No thank you."

He went back into the kitchen. She continued to watch him carefully as he poured his coffee. Maybe he should let her get to the point of her visit so she'd leave and get could go back to bed. He carried his coffee back into the living room and sat down opposite her again.

"Okay. What did you want to talk about?"

"You were with her night before last. I wondered … I mean, did she give you anything to … to kind of look after?"

"No," said James and it occurred to him that he'd forgotten where he'd hidden the envelope last night.

"I mean, if she was here, she might have just left it without telling you."

"She wasn't here." Maybe he should ask her how she found out he was with Megan, but if he started asking questions, he'd probably start to get some answers and one thing would lead to another and all of a sudden he'd become involved all over again, which he needed like a hole in the head right now.

"You *did* go out with her, didn't you?"

"No," said James.

"But I thought." She let it trail off, inviting James to get her off the hook. He didn't. The silence between them grew. She really was an extremely pretty girl, decided James. She was wearing a fashionably short skirt which showed most of her legs, including a flash of underwear when she adjusted her position on the sofa. If she'd been ten years older, with a little more meat on her bones, he might have made a pass at her. Old habits die hard. But right now, all he wanted was for her to leave. He stood up.

"Listen, if there is nothing else, I've got work to do."

She didn't move, except to grope in her purse for a tissue which she used to mop the silent tears which had started to run down her face.

James considered sitting down again, then changed his mind. She would probably consider it a sign of encouragement and start to tell him why she was crying. He didn't want to know why she as crying. It was none of his business and he aimed to keep it that way. And if she thought a few tears were going to soften him up, then she had another thing coming to her. He was immune. Nevertheless, he couldn't just stand there. He went to top up his coffee cup. He stayed in the kitchen area until he heard her blow her nose loudly, a sign that the crisis was over. Only then did he come back into the living room. She was examining herself in a small hand mirror she'd taken from her purse.

"May I use your bathroom?" she asked.

James pointed her towards the bedroom and the bathroom beyond. She disappeared to repair her mascara. He stayed where he was, still trying to remember where he'd hidden the envelope.

She was back five minutes later. "I'm sorry," she said. "I did not mean to make a spectacle of myself."

"You didn't," James said.

"It's just that Megan had something that belonged to Daddy and I've just got to find it."

"Why?"

"Why what?"

"Why is it so important that you find it?"

"Oh … it's not really. It's just … well it's family … you know." She was a terrible liar. "I really don't know why I should have imagined that she'd have given it to you."

"Right," said James.

"I mean … you didn't even know her all that well, did you?"

"Nope."

"It's not like you were good friends."

"No, it's not."

"Even acquaintances?"

"Even so," said James.

Obviously, fishing was going to get her no place. She looked at him helplessly for a moment, almost as it she might start to cry again. Then she shot off on a different tack entirely. "Your bedroom is a terrible mess."

No carpet, an unmade bed, probably still with bloodstains he'd overlooked, a buckled shelf drawer, also bloodstained. Yeah, terrible mess seemed to cover it.

"Sure is," said James. "Now, if there's nothing else."

This time it worked. She slumped within herself and headed past him towards the front door. He caught a whiff of her perfume as she brushed by him. He was a sucker for perfume. Hers was virginal and sexy at the same time. But at his time of life, virginal was sexy.

"I'm sorry to have troubled you," she said, from the door.

"No trouble," said James. "Sorry I couldn't help."

Her silk blouse had lost a button. Strange he hadn't noticed it before. He could see the inner slopes of her breasts, firm and high. She really was a remarkably pretty girl, not nearly as skinny as he had first imagined. Great legs, too.

"Maybe I should have your phone number just in case something comes up," he said. Something was already coming up and he was hating himself because of it. Why did he always feel so horny when he had a hangover?

"Like what?"

"You never know, I might remember something that could be useful to you. I mean, I didn't *know* your stepmother but at least I *met* her a couple of times."

She thought about this for a moment before obviously deciding it wasn't a good idea.

"There wouldn't be any point, I'm going home this afternoon. Back east."

Just as well, thought James, commonsense overwhelming temporary lust. He needed an involvement with a child/woman right now like he needed a lobotomy.

He stood at the door of the guest house, watching her let herself out of the front gate. He didn't even hear Landers come up behind him from the main house.

"What are you Reed, some kind of a dirty old man?" There was an ache of envy in his voice.

"It was business," said James.

"Sure, such business I should be having."

"What do you want, Mr. Landers?"

"What do I want? I want my landlord who's charging me ten thousand dollars a month, to fix the washer and the dryer. I want my landlord to pay some attention when I tell him things what ain't right. And I want him to fix them sometime before we all die of old age. That's what I want Mr. Landlord." The dialogue was the same, but his mind was on other things. "What kind of business is a little girl like that involved in? Maybe she needs a partner."

"You're the dirty old man, Mr. Landers."

"It's not my house she's coming out of at the crack of dawn."

"You're right Mr. Landers. I'm a dirty old man. She's sixteen and she's been sleeping over. Except we didn't sleep, we rolled around the bedroom all night doing disgusting things to each other."

"I don't believe you," said Landers.

"So, look in the bedroom," said James.

Landers walked past him into the guesthouse. James came in after him and went to the kitchen to fetch himself a fresh cup of coffee. As he came back into the living room, Landers came out of the bedroom. He was pink cheeked with excitement and embarrassment.

"I'm sorry," he said. "I didn't know. I was joking."

"Forget it," said James.

"You should have told me to mind my own business."

"Don't worry about it."

"It's embarrassing, I'm ashamed of myself." He started towards the front door. Before he went out, he turned back. "What do you do with the metal drawer for God's sake?"

"I'll tell you later," said James.

"Please, I'd rather not know."

He left, no doubt to tell Mrs. Landers that their landlord was a child molester.

James tried again to remember where he'd put the envelope. It wasn't in any of the normal places… drawers, behind books, back of shelves. He must have been even drunker than he remembered. It took him twenty minutes to find it. It was in the garbage. That meant he must have emptied out the garage last night, put the envelope in the can and replaced the garbage on top of it. Maybe he was hitting the booze a shade too hard. But what the hell, it wasn't more than a couple of times a week. And he *had* quit smoking. He scraped the envelope clean and examined it again. It hadn't changed from last night. He was still going to have to rip it open if he wanted to know what it contained. Better he hadn't found it. Better he'd thrown it out with the garbage, because now he was going to have to make a decision and he wasn't into decision making right now. And why should this morning be any different than last night? He'd decided then that he didn't want to know what the envelope contained. Now, just because a slip of a girl had caught him with his hormones down, all of a sudden, he was about to get involved. Better judgement told him to go with his last night's decision, dump the envelope and forget it ever existed. He poured himself another cup of coffee, stiffened it with a large scotch and fetched the letter opener.

It wasn't a notebook or a cassette or a computer disc. It was a key, taped between a couple of pieces of thick cardboard. There was a number embossed on the key: 39.

James had seen keys like this before. It belonged to a locker at an airport or a bus terminal or a railroad station. He got up and went to pour himself another cup of coffee. The pot was empty. He started to make fresh pot, then he changed his mind. What he really needed right now was to clear some of the cobwebs out of his skull. He pulled on a track suit stuffed the key in his pocket and went for a stagger on the beach.

He was whacked on the side of the head by a frisbee; a dog snapped at his heels for a couple of hundred yards; and a hysterical mother yelled at him for kicking sand in her child's face. But he cleared his head. As he let himself in through the gate, he heard his name called from the terrace of the main house. It was Mrs. Landers.

She was leaning over the railing looking down at him, her vast bosom threatening to overbalance her. This was the first time James had seen her outside the house. It wasn't a pretty sight.

"How are you Mrs. Landers?" No point in not being polite.

"Surviving, Mr. Reed, surviving. Bernard and I were wondering if you'd like to come to supper tonight."

"That's kind of you Mrs. Landers, but I'm busy tonight."

She looked disappointed. It wasn't every day you got a chance to meet a child molester socially.

"Some other time, maybe," she called after him as he went up the path at the side of the main house.

He showered. He tidied up the bedroom, finding some bloodstains on the wall which he hadn't noticed before. Then he examined the key again. It was still just a key. Number 39. He examined the two pieces of stiff cardboard the key had been taped between. He rechecked the envelope. None of it told him anything. There was only one solution to the problem. Find the locker that the key fitted, open it and see what everybody was getting so hot about. He gave it some serious thought for a couple of minutes before remembering that he didn't care. All he *did* care about was not being involved with the dead woman, her stepdaughter, two crazy hoods, whoever was paying their wages and, last but not least, the LAPD in the shape of Lieutenant Micklehaus, who chose that moment to call on the phone.

"It wasn't the husband," he said without preamble.

"How do you know?"

"Because the husband is in New York."

"Guaranteed?"

"Copper bottomed," said Micklehaus.

"Did you find the shamus?"

"He says he didn't employ no shamus."

"You believe him?"

"He's got no interest in his ex-wife. Haven't been in touch with her for at least twelve months. Why should he need a shamus? Which brings us to the question, who was following the two of you last night?"

"Search me," said James.

"Maybe you dreamed it up."

Micklehaus didn't believe him, so fuck Micklehaus. Maybe it had been Patsy following them. But there was no way he was going to tell Micklehaus. The kid was in enough of a bind already.

"You must have been a lousy cop back when," said Micklehaus.

"At least I had the good sense to quit, lieutenant"

Micklehaus mumbled something that could have been "Fuck you" and told James it would be okay for him to leave town if he wanted.

James didn't want, but he was curious. "How come?"

"I been doing some checking. It doesn't figure that you offed her but do me a favor. You want to leave town, okay, but let me know where you're going."

James promised to keep the police informed of his future movements and hung up. Okay, so now he was done with the whole affair. He'd told nearly all the truth to nearly all the people involved. He was home and dry, with a clean slate. No need to ask any more questions or follow any leads because none of it was any of his business. Megan McCoy had gotten herself killed and he'd gotten beat up slightly. Could have happened to anyone. Except he was out $2000 already. Add in another grand that it would cost before he'd finished redecorating the bedroom, and a couple more to compensate for the bruising and the aggravation he'd going through. Say $5000 in all. He called the phone company and asked to speak to a supervisor.

"I'm terribly sorry, but I wonder if you could do me a great favor?" he asked

The supervisor wasn't accustomed to such politeness, especially when it was delivered in a broad English accent. She promised to do what she could to help.

"I knew you would," said James, "You Americans are all so kind and helpful it makes me quite ashamed to be English. You're going to think me an awful ninny, but I made a couple of calls to a friend of mine out-of-town yesterday and then, silly me, I went and lost his number. I know you people keep a record of every call that's made because it appears on those incredibly efficient bills you send out, not like back home where they just ask you for money without any finesse whatsoever. Anyway, I wonder if you could pull me up on your computer, or whatever it is you have to do, and let me have the number of my friend. I called him twice, first time about noon and the second fifteen or twenty minutes later."

The supervisor established that she wasn't supposed to give out that kind of information over the line, that she could get the sack for doing so and possibly lose her pension rights. Then, having established what a huge favor she was doing, she asked James to hang on. She was back thirty seconds later with the number Gary and Bill had called. It was a 212 number.

"That's a Manhattan number isn't it?" asked James.

"I really don't have that information I'm sorry."

"It's terribly important. You see, I think my friend is going to kill himself. I need the number of the police station closest to his address so they can send somebody round there right away."

She went off the line for a few seconds, then came back on and gave him another number which she assured him was for the police precinct house closest to his friend's place. She wished him luck with his life saving mission before hanging up. James called the police number she'd given him and asked to speak to whoever was on duty.

"Sergeant Rodrigues, whaddayawant?"

"Some guy just called me and told me he was going to kill himself," said James.

"So?"

"So, I want you to send someone round to stop him."

"Who am I talkin' to?"

"The Good Shepherds of Manhattan," said James.

"Never heard of you. What are you? Like the Samaritans?"

"Something like that," said James. "Now are you gonna go round and stop this guy taking a dive from the top floor of his building?"

"We're real busy right now, buddy."

"We're trained to deal with cases like this ourselves, but I don't have his name or address, just his phone number."

"What is it?"

James told him, Rodriguez asked him to hold on. He came back two minutes later.

"You'll take care of it, right?"

"Give me his name and address and you can forget you ever heard from me," said James.

"It's an unlisted number so I shouldn't be telling you this."

"So, take care of it yourself," said James, "Good bye."

"Wait! The phone is in the name Webber, Penthouse 5, High Tower, that's on Fifth." Rodriguez suddenly thought of something. "Say he takes a dive from there, he'll snarl traffic for a week."

"You know the building?" asked James.

"Sure. I know it. What's a guy who can afford to live in High Tower got to kill himself over?"

"Maybe they just put up his rent," said James.

So now he had a name and address. He'd offer to sell Webber the key for the $5000 price tag he'd put on it. A straightforward commercial transaction. He didn't know why the key was so important and he didn't care. He was still telling himself this as he picked up the phone and again and dialed Webber's number in New York.

"This is the Webber residence," answer a plummy voice. It could have been an answering service but James just knew it was a butler.

"I'd like to speak to Mr. Webber please," English accent once more, it often impressed the help.

"Whom shall I say is calling?"

"James Reed."

"Hold the line please whilst I ascertain whether or not Mr. Webber is available."

James held the line. It seemed that Mr. Webber was available. He came on the line about a minute later.

"Mr. Reed, do I know you?"

"Sure, you do Mr. Webber or you wouldn't be talking to me."

"What can I do for you?" His voice was pleasant, even over the telephone, well-modulated, with the flat accent that came from being born and brought up in the eastern United States and educated there and in Europe. It was the voice of one of those rare features, a truly sophisticated American.

"You can send me $5000," said James.

There was a slight pause. "Why should I do that?" Still very reasonable.

"Because if you do, I might let you have the package everyone's so hot to get their hands on."

"The package you told my people you didn't have, that package?"

"Believe me, when I told them I didn't have it I was telling the truth."

"But now you do."

"Yes sir, now I do."

"You've opened it of course."

"Of course."

"And?"

"It's a key."

"Ahh." James detected an edge of relief. Obviously, he'd been expecting something else. "Can you be more specific a key to what?"

"To a public locker."

"Located where?"

"I haven't the faintest idea. Maybe you do?"

Webber ignored the implied question, "You said 'everyone' wants the package, who else has been looking for it?"

"Just a figure of speech, Mr. Webber." No point in telling him about Patsy.

He seemed to accept this evasion.

"And you want $5000 for it."

"To cover the damages."

"What damages?"

"To my home and to my peace of mind. The two bruisers will tell you about it as soon as they get out of the hospital."

He heard a chuckle across the line. "You sound like a resourceful man, Mr. Reed. Which you most certainly need to be if you've angered those men."

"If I was resourceful, I'd be asking fifty thousand instead of five."

"What makes you think it's worth that much to me?"

"The trouble you've gone through to get your hands on it."

"All right, I admit it's quite important to me. How did you get my name and number incidentally?"

"You said it yourself, I'm resourceful. Is it a deal?"

"It's a deal. How do you want your money?"

"In cash. You can arrange that?"

"Of course."

"I'll turn the key over to whoever brings me the money."

"Tomorrow." There was a moment's pause. "Mr. Reed, did you kill Megan McCoy?"

"No. Did you?"

"No. Aren't you interested in who was responsible?"

"Not particularly, are you?

"As a matter of fact, I think I might know who did it."

"Then I suppose you'll tell the police."

"Perhaps you'll do it for me. I'll give you the information you need."

"Why do you need a go-between?"

"I'd prefer not to have my name mixed up in this."

"I imagine you would Mr. Webber," said James. He hung up.

Okay, so I'm an avaricious, greedy son of a bitch, he thought. He'd seen the chance to pick up five grand and he'd jumped at it. He tried it on for size using the mirror behind the bar.

"You're a greedy avaricious son of a bitch," he said to his reflection.

But his reflection knew him better than that.

"Maybe you are buddy, but that's not your real problem. Your real problem is that you're vindictive and bloody-minded and you don't like the idea of anybody getting away with anything even if you haven't the vaguest notion of what it is they're getting away with, right?"

"Right," said James.

"Jesus Christ, talking to yourself now?" Landers was standing just outside the open front door.

"What is it Mr. Landers?"

Landers looked at him for a long moment.

"You wanna know something? I forgot. Seeing you jabbering away at yourself like that put it clear out of my mind."

"Maybe when you remember, you'll let me know."

"Yeah. Sure." He peered into the guest house without actually crossing the threshold.

"She's not here," said James.

"Who?" His innocence was total.

"Lolita."

"Never crossed my mind," said Landers. He looked disappointed. After a couple of seconds more, during which he continued to look at James, he shook his head sadly and started back towards the main house.

James went to the front door and called after him. "Mr. Landers, you're a New Yorker, right?"

"So?" Landers was suspicious.

James pulled the key from his pocket and flipped it towards Landers who caught it. "Ever see a key like that before?"

"It's for a locker. Grand Central, Kennedy Airport. The Bus Station. One of those."

"Any idea which one?"

"I might be able to find out."

James was impressed, "How?"

"Friend of mine, Abe Schiner, we play gin most Mondays. He's in the lock and key business in New York. That's a good business to be in, believe you me. If anyone knows where that key belongs, it'll be Abe. You want I should call him?"

"Maybe later, Mr. Landers. Thanks," James held out his hand for the key.

Landers looked disappointed. "That's it?"

"It is unless you've heard of a man named Webber."

"There's a lot of Webbers. There's Hank who runs a deli on Seventh at 45th who serves pastrami like you used to get in the old days. There's a guy called Webber runs a book out back of his hardware store on Columbus up in the nineties. I know a Webber used to be an undertaker 'til he died. Take your pick."

"Webber who lives in Penthouse 5, High Tower on Fifth Avenue?"

"That Webber I don't know."

"I didn't think you would," said James.

"I heard of them though," said Landers.

"You're putting me on," said James.

"Everybody's heard of Jackson Webber, unless he's a schmuck," said Landers. He was starting to enjoy himself.

"Okay, so I'm a schmuck, tell me about Jackson Webber."

"You heard of Donald Trump."

"Even schmucks have heard of Trump."

"Okay, so picture a Donald Trump with class and you've got Jackson Webber. He got rich the same way Trump did, but he did it better and he did it quieter and he didn't do it in New York. He did it in Chicago and Boston and Detroit and Seattle. The only thing he did in New York was to build himself a high rise like Trump. But he didn't go hanging his own name on it. I told you, he's got class. He called it High Tower. And when they wanted to put his face on the front of *Time Magazine,* he told them no thank you very much, I don't need it."

"How come you know all this, Mr. Landers?"

"I read the newspapers. I listen to the gossip at my club."

"What club is that?"

"You wouldn't know my club, Mr. Reed, we don't allow goyim. It's an exclusive place, even for Jews. You gotta have ten million in the bank to get in the front door. Even then they treat you like you was a nobody."

"You've got ten million in the bank?"

Landers shrugged, "Give or take a dollar or two."

"So how come you've been behaving like a pain the ass over a lousy one day's rent?"

"If I didn't worry about such things, maybe I wouldn't have ten million dollars in the bank. Now I'll see you later, once I remember what I came here to complain about. And if you want to know anything more about New York or Jackson Webber or locker keys, you know where to find me."

He headed back towards the main house looking more chipper than James had ever seen him. James went back into the guest house. He'd been having a conversation with himself when Landers had shown up. He wasn't finished with it yet. And because it was 11 a.m., he made himself a Bloody Mary.

❧   ❧   ❧

Micklehaus called him before he'd even added the Worcester Sauce.

"You want to get your ass down here under your own steam or you should I send somebody to bring you in?"

"What's your problem, lieutenant?"

"Right now, you're my problem. How come you didn't tell me about Paul Menzies?"

"What was I supposed to tell you?"

"How it was him who introduced you to McCoy woman, how it was him who was banging her brains out; how it was—"

"Hold on there, Lieutenant, Paul Menzies was screwing Megan McCoy?

"Like a tomcat. And don't sound so goddamned surprised."

"Who told you all this?"

"None of your business. Just get on down here."

"I'm not going any place, Micklehaus. You want to ask me some questions you come on down here or do it over the phone."

There was a long pause at the other end of the line. James let it draw out. He was in no hurry.

"Okay," said Micklehaus finally. "Where does Paul Menzies fit into all this?"

"Why don't you ask him?"

"I would if I could find him, but I can't, so I'm asking you."

James told him everything he knew about Paul, which, on reflection, was remarkably little.

"That's it?"

"That's it."

Micklehaus hung up without another word. Thirty seconds later the phone rang again. James picked it up, "I won't leave town," he said.

"Mr. Reed, this is Paul Menzies."

"The law is on your tail Paul."

"I know it. You said you wouldn't tell."

"I didn't. And I just got my ass reamed because of it. Somebody else has been shooting off their mouth."

"You and me have got to talk."

"What about?"

"Important stuff, Mr. Reed. Like who killed Megan."

"They think it was you."

"Yeah, that's why I've gotta skip town. I figured if you and I could have a talk I'd tell you some stuff that'll help point the finger at who did it. That way I can lay low until you steer the law to the guy."

"Better you turn yourself in. If you didn't do it, you've got nothing to worry about," said James, not believing it for a moment.

Paul didn't either. "No way. So where can we meet up?"

"I don't think I want to do that, Paul."

"Don't throw me to the sharks, Mr. Reed. I didn't do it but I'm not gonna be able to prove it without some help. You're the only friend I got."

If I'm his only friend, he's in deep shit, thought James. On the other hand, the very fact that he was making this call went a long way towards proving he was telling the truth. "Okay Paul, I'm not promising anything, but I'll listen to what you've got to say."

"That's all I'm asking, Mr. Reed. The law's got the tennis club all staked out, but if you go along Malibu Canyon a couple more miles, you come to a place where the road goes under the mountain. A tunnel. Pull of the road just the other side of the tunnel, I'll meet you there. Can you make it half an hour from now?

James promised he'd be there. He spent the next five minutes wondering how he could change his mind without letting Paul down. He decided he couldn't. He escaped from the house one jump ahead of Landers who had obviously found out what he was supposed to have complained about earlier. As he drove off, he left Landers stranded out front of the house enveloped in dirty exhaust smoke.

If the tennis club was being staked out, the police were doing it from the inside. There were no visible signs of the law from the highway. As Paul said, a couple of miles further on, a long straight stretch of road suddenly went into a short tunnel about a hundred feet long. James did as he'd been asked and pulled off the road as he emerged from the tunnel. He killed the engine and, without getting out of the car, tried to see where Paul was hiding himself. After five minutes, he decided he'd come on a fool's errand. Paul wasn't going to show, which was okay with him because he'd been regretting the impulse to meet ever since he had hung up the telephone. He started the car again and prepared to make the U-turn back onto the highway. At that moment, he saw Paul. He was slithering down the steep, rocky hill above the tunnel. Paul reached the highway and hurried towards James's car. James leaned across and opened the passenger door for him. Paul climbed in and slammed the door after him. For somebody who was being hunted for a murder, he looked in remarkably good shape.

"You thought I'd bring the law, right?" said James.

Paul looked hurt and innocent, "No sir, why should you think that?"

"You weren't sitting on top of that mountain enjoying the view."

Paul tried on a grin. He was ready to snatch it back if it wasn't acceptable. He was so eager to please that James felt like a bastard for challenging him.

"Okay, Mr. Reed. You're right. It's not that I don't trust you, I thought maybe the police might be following you without knowing about it."

James didn't believe a word of it, but he didn't argue. "So, I'm here. Talk to me."

"Can we drive someplace where I can get some food, I haven't eaten since yesterday."

"Where do you want to go?"

"I don't want to go back to the beach. That's where they'll be looking for me."

"If they're looking for you, they'll be doing it all over," said James. "The way you're dressed you'll stand out everyplace *but* the beach …" Paul was wearing shorts and a tee shirt.

"I didn't think of that," said Paul.

"Sounds to me there's a lot you didn't think about," said James. He started the car, made a U-turn back onto the highway and headed back towards the coast.

Paul didn't say a word until they were passing the entrance to the tennis club. "I'm gonna miss that place" he said. "First regular job I ever had. You never did get me that autographed photo of your ex-wife you promised me."

"You've got a bit of a priority problem, Paul."

"How's that Mr. Reed?"

He was so innocent it was frightening. "You've got more important things to worry about right now than tennis clubs and movie star photos."

"Yeah, you're right. But I ain't gonna worry too much, long as you're helping me, I figure it'll work out okay."

"We'd better get something straight, Paul. I'm not laying myself open to accessory charges, obstructing justice, any of that shit. I'll feed you and I'll listen to what you've got to say. Depending on what this is, I might even take you to the bus station afterwards. On the other hand, I might turn you over to the law myself. Understood?"

"Sure, Mr. Reed, anything you say."

James could tell by the tone in Paul's voice and by the way he relaxed back in the passenger seat, that Paul Menzies didn't have a worry in the world because Mr. Reed was going to take care of every little thing.

Just in case Paul had been right and the police were looking for him along the coast highway, James took him home to feed him. He told Paul that if Landers suddenly turned up, Paul should pretend to be a guy being interviewed with a view to painting the house or mending the roof or some such. Apart from Landers, James didn't expect to be disturbed. He turned Paul loose in the kitchen to help himself to whatever he could find while he fetched himself a drink. He drew a stool up to the kitchen counter and watched Paul scramble half a dozen eggs, dump in a can of tomatoes, a can of red peppers and then start to complain because James didn't have any tortillas to pita or just plain bread.

"You don't start talking soon, you're gonna be doing your complaining from San Quentin," said James finally.

"No sir," said Paul, with his mouth full. "No way I'm going to jail."

"I wouldn't bet on it."

"You would if you knew me better." He emptied a carton of milk in what looked like one long swallow.

"So, tell me how you plan to stay free, barring hiding out in my bedroom closet for the rest of your life."

Paul grinned at him as he shoveled in another mouthful of eggs and whatever. "I like you Mr. Reed. I liked you from when we first met. Remember, that night on the beach when those …."

"I remember for Christ's sake. Now get on with it."

"Sorry." He looked like a large puppy dog who'd been mildly scolded. "Okay, what do you want to know?"

"Holy shit, Paul, you asked to meet me because you had, and I quote, 'all kinds of important stuff' to tell me, right?"

"Right, okay, first I didn't kill Mrs. McCoy."

"Any particular reason I should believe you?"

"'Cause I'm telling the truth."

"Why didn't you tell me you and she were having an affair?"

"Who told you that?"

"The police. I assume it's true."

"Sure it's true, least it *was* true. It was a while back. That's why she came out here. I told her back east we didn't have a future together. I mean, I really told her. I told her I was coming out here and there weren't no point in her following me because we were through. Sure, I still liked her and I respected her, but a guy's gotta make it on his own sometime. I told her she wasn't to follow me. What does she do? She finds out where I'm located and next thing I know, here she is, banging on my door and wanting to start over just where we left off. I tell her we been through all that and she tells me that now it's different. How's it different I ask her. She tells me and that's when I really tell her to get out of my life." He looked around, "Where's the bathroom?"

James nodded towards the bedroom. He fetched himself another drink while Paul was in the bathroom.

Paul came back into the living room. "Your bedroom's a mess," he said. "You want I should redecorate it for you, lay some carpet, fix the dresser? I'm pretty handy at stuff like that."

"All I want is for you to keep on talking," said James.

Paul found himself some ice cream James didn't even remember he had and started eating it straight from the carton. "Okay, where was I?"

"You were telling Megan McCoy to get out of your life for the second time."

"Right, like I said, she was a nice enough lady, and maybe I could have taken up with her again. I was pretty lonely out here and we had some fun times together. She told me we didn't have to worry about money no more. She was always a bit short back home I mean, after the divorce and all, she didn't get much from Mr. McCoy. Far as I could make out, all the money she had was what she earned in her job. Not that I ran out on her because of the money, you understand. But maybe that's the way she figured it. Anyway, here she was, back again, telling me there were gonna be no more money problems. So how come, I asked her? She gets a bit cagey. You don't want to know, she said. I want to know or I'd not be asking I say, so she tells me." He finished the ice cream and looked in the freezer to see if there was more. He looked disappointed when he didn't find any.

"So, tell me," said James.

"Okay, it seems she'd got some stuff on the guy she was working for. The kind of stuff he'd pay for her to keep quiet about. I told her, that's blackmail. I said, you can go to jail for blackmail. No way was she going to jail, she said, her boss would pay up and that would be an end of it. She'd have enough money for the two of us to go off someplace and get married and raise a family. I couldn't believe it. She was near old enough to be my mother, for Pete's sake. I didn't tell her that of course. I just told her I didn't leave her the first time because she didn't have any money and I sure as hell wasn't going back with her given it had been honest made money, which this wasn't gonna be."

"What did she do?"

"She made a bit of a fuss. You know how it is, cried a bit, told me I was nothing but a bum and always would be unless I let her stay in my life. You know, all the usual shit they can hand you when they think you've lost the hots for them. I told her that was it, final, so long and good bye. I didn't even know she was dead for Christ's sake until you came and told me."

"Why don't you tell that to the police?"

"You think they'd believe me? I've been in and out of her hotel four or five times. The staff there have heard her yelling at me and me yelling back at her. Shit man, one night we went back there after having dinner and we'd been arguing in the car and she keeps on arguing as we go through the lobby and just before she gets in the elevator she tells me to go fuck myself and she hauls off and hits me right there in front of everybody."

"How many times you hit her?"

"I've never hit a lady in my life, Mr. Reed. No sir, the only way I'm gonna get off the hook is for them to nail the real killer."

"Any ideas?"

"It has to be the guy she was getting ready to blackmail; I mean, it stands to reason."

"You know who he is?"

"Sure, I know. Webber's his name. Jackson Webber. He's a big wheel from back east. I mean a very big wheel. Top family, always going to the opera and the concerts and those other things they do at the Lincoln Center. Him and his wife are heavy into charity work. Their picture's always in the newspaper. He's got more money than you or I could even dream about. Me, anyway, I don't know about you Mr. Reed."

"Me, too, Paul," said James.

"Anyway, Megan was working for him, kind of as a social secretary. The way I see it, if Megan's got something on him, he'd want her out of the way."

"What would she have on him that could be so important?"

"I dunno, a guy like that. Maybe she just threatened to tell the wife she and her old man have been having it off. It would sure fuck up his social image if it got out he was banging his secretary."

James doubted it. Most men banged their secretaries sooner or later.

But Paul hadn't finished. "Course he wouldn't do it himself. No sir, not Mr. Jackson Webber esquire. He's got these two creeps who work for him. Couple of fags, but mean motherfuckers, take my word for it. They do the dirty work. He's likely to get them to do it."

"How do you know about them?"

"He sent them round to see me once, when I was in Spring Lake. They told me stop messing with Megan 'cause Mr. Webber, their boss, didn't like somebody dipping his bucket in the same well."

"Didn't you mind that somebody else was screwing your lady friend?"

"Why should I mind? Funny thing though, I told Megan, cool, no sweat, but she got really pissed off at me not minding. There she was, screwing this guy and when I tell her okay, *she* gave me a hard time. Anyway, these two creeps told me to lay off or they'd break some of my bones. I told them to get lost so they tried pushing me around some to show they meant business."

"They hurt you?"

"I don't push easy, Mr. Reed. I sent 'em packing with fleas in their ears."

He wasn't boasting. It was an encounter that James would deeply have loved to have witnessed.

"Still and all," Paul went on, "There's no lady worth getting beat up over, and like, while I can take care of myself most of the time, I don't want a couple of heavyweight fags creeping up on me some dark night when I'm not looking and beating my brains out, which they'd enjoy doing, believe you me."

"I believe you," said James.

"That's when I told Megan I was on my way. She kicked up all kinds of fuss. She figured I was walking out on her because I found out she was screwing around with Webber. I told her she could screw around with anyone she wanted, me walking out was so I'd stay in one piece, thanks very much. She said she'd quit her job with Webber and stop seeing him. I said for her to forget it 'cause there was no way I was gonna get any bones broken over her or anybody else. She said we could go off someplace where he wouldn't find us and I told her sure, what are we gonna use for money. It was goin' back and forth like that for a few days 'til, in the end I just packed my bag and hopped a ride out here."

"How did she find you?"

"Search me."

There'd been a fractional pause, enough for James to know he was lying. "Okay, that's it. On your bike."

"Hey man, what did I do?"

"Out. I'll give you thirty minutes head start before I call the police."

"Okay, okay." He looked like an overgrown schoolboy caught cheating in class. "She found out through Patsy, that's her stepdaughter."

"How did Patsy know where to find you?"

Paul shrugged. "I called her a couple of times when I got out here. Her and me, we had a little something going on between us."

"You were banging her too?"

"On and off. It was no big deal. Anyway, I told her where I was at, in case she wanted to come out here for a visit. I guess that's how Megan found out because the next thing I know she shows up."

"Megan?"

"Sure Megan."

"Patsy didn't arrive until later?"

"Patsy didn't arrive at all."

"I've got news for you," said James. "She was here yesterday."

"You're putting me on."

"Suit yourself," said James. He went to freshen up his Bloody Mary.

"You drink too much, Mr. Reed. It'll rot your liver."

"Quit worrying about my state of health. You're the one who's in a bind," said James. "Tell me about Patsy."

He shrugged, "What's to tell, I didn't know she was here. What did she want?"

"What everyone else seems to want."

It took a couple of seconds for it to sink in, but finally got there. "The stuff Megan was gonna use to blackmail Mr. Webber. What would she want with that shit?"

"She said it belonged to her father."

"Maybe there's something in it that points the finger at her daddy. He and Mr. Webber had business dealings. Megan told me that once."

"What kind of business dealings?"

"Search me."

"Think about it."

Paul thought about it. "Maybe it has something to do with Patsy's daddy working for city hall."

"What does he do?"

'Shit, I don't know. Yes, I do, he's an architect. Megan told me once. He designed the extension they put on back of their house at Spring Lake. She said could you believe a professional working architect designing a piece of shit extension like that? It looked pretty good from where I was standing but what do I know?"

He knew a hell of a lot more than he was letting on, though. "What do you want me to do, Paul?"

"I told you, point the finger at the guy who did so's the law will know which way is up for a change."

"They figure they already know which way is up. Look at it from their point of view. A guy beat up his lady in a Beverly Hills parking lot because she's going out with another guy. Then he hangs around and follows her and her date and when she gets back to the hotel, he goes up to room and knocks her around a bit more, only this time it gets out of hand and he winds up killing her. Sounds like a pretty good scenario to me."

Paul looked genuinely puzzled. "You lost me there Mr. Reed."

"Didn't you beat her up in the parking lot the night she and I had a date?"

"Not me, I didn't even know you two had a date. How was it?"

"How was what?"

"The date?"

"It was a load of laughs. She got herself killed."

"If you were with her the night she was murdered, it's a wonder the cops aren't after you, too."

"I've got an alibi," said James, the lie coming easily.

"Yeah, well, some guys got luck."

"Meaning you haven't?"

"I spent that night in a sleeping bag at the club. The guy I'm sharing a room with had something going for him and asked me to get lost."

"What the name of this guy?"

Paul looked a little sheepish. "Okay, it's not a guy, it's a chick. She's got a pad a bit further up the canyon from the club. When her boyfriend's out of town, she lets me sleep over."

"Pretty generous with your cock, aren't you?" said James, trying to keep the envy out of his voice.

"You know how it is," said Paul. "Anyway, I was on my own from about eight through the following morning."

"I still don't know what you think I can do to help," said James. "Or why you think I should even be bothered."

"I told you, you're the only friend I've got out here."

"What about the girl you've been staying with?"

"Come on, Mr. Reed, she's not a friend. She's just a chick. She gives me a bed some nights when she's lonely. No sir, you're it, if you don't help me, that's it. There's no way I'm going to jail. What do you say Mr. Reed?" He looked more like an overgrown puppy than ever.

"I'll think about it," said James.

"How long?"

"I'll let you know. Where are you going to be?"

"I don't know. Back east. They won't be looking for me so hard back there."

"How are you going to get there?"

"I'll hitch, the same way I got here."

"You need any money?"

"A couple of bucks would be a real help, Mr. Reed."

James gave him twenty-five dollars, all the cash he had. He'd liked to have given him more, because he'd already decided it was all that Paul Menzies was going to get out of him. There was nothing he could do to help. He wasn't going to shop him to Micklehaus, but that was as far as it went. Eventually, the law would catch up with him, at which time James would do everything he could for him, bar baking a cake with a hacksaw file in it. Hopefully, by then, other evidence would come to light which would point the finger in another direction, maybe at Webber's men, maybe at somebody that no one had even thought of.

Paul took the twenty-five dollars gratefully. James walked him out of the guesthouse, suggesting that he leave along the beach. Just before he left, Paul stuck out his hand for James to shake.

"I want to thank you from the bottom of my heart, Mr. Reed. I don't know what I'd do if it wasn't for you." James took the proffered hand and Paul dragged him close and threw his other arm around his back, hugging him hard for a moment. "You're a real friend," he said, his voice choking up. Then he released James and ran down the path at the side of the main house that led to the beach.

James was about to go back into the house when he saw Landers. His tenant was standing a few feet away, half-hidden behind the corner of the garage. As James looked towards him, he ducked back into cover.

"You want something Mr. Landers?"

Landers stepped into the clear since he'd been spotted. "What is it with you Mr. Reed? Boys and girls, makes no difference, coming in and out of your apartment at all hours, hugging and kissing. What kind of den of vice have you got going for yourself in there?"

"You want to do me a big favor, Mr. Landers?"

Landers looked suspicious and eager at the same time. Maybe the landlord was going to ask him to join in some of the depravities that were obviously taking place in the guest house. "What kind of favor?"

"That boy you just saw leaving here ...."

"What about him?"

"Anybody asks, you didn't see him."

"If you say so," said Landers. He looked past James towards the guest house. "You got anybody else in there? Some animals, maybe?"

"You want to come in and find out?" said James with a leer.

Landers recoiled. "All I want from you, Mr. Reed, is that you get somebody to check out the hot water."

"What's the matter with it?"

"It's not hot is what's the matter with it. Ten thousand dollars a month, a pervert for a landlord and no hot water. I gotta be *meshuga*."

James drove to the shopping center at the end of the beach road where he told the guy in the hardware store to make him a key that more or less resembled the locker key. It didn't have to fit the same lock. In fact, James insisted that it didn't. It just had to look similar with the number 39 embossed on it. The guy who cut the key knew James, so he simply did as he was told without asking any questions.

As long as James was at the shopping center, he went to the market and bought himself some smoked salmon and a couple of steaks for dinner, along with a case of cheap but cheerful wine He was coming into some unexpected money tomorrow. Tonight, he'd celebrate.

Back home, he got out his little black book and tried to decide who the lucky lady of the evening was going to be. He was still trying to make up his mind when there was knock on the door.

"Come in Mr. Landers," he called.

Landers came in. He took a quick look around the door. "You alone?"

"The orgy doesn't start until later," said James.

"Yeah, well maybe you can fix my hot water first."

James had forgotten about the hot water. "Can't it wait until tomorrow?"

"No way. Becky wants to take a bath, I want to take a bath, Carmelita needs to take a bath. We need hot water. And for ten grand-a-month, I figure we're entitled."

"You're right, Mr. Landers, you're entitled."

James followed him back to the main house where he spent ten minutes locating the problem. The pilot in the furnace had gone out. It had happened before and it was no big deal. He relit it and told Landers in half-an-hour they could all bathe to their heart's content. Back in the guest house, he started to leaf through his address book once more. Then he decided the hell with it, he didn't want to cook supper for anybody after all, not even himself. He stuck the steaks in the freezer and drove to the Randy Tar, a local watering hole, where the food and drink didn't cost too much and where the assistant manager was a lady who he vaguely fancied and who had started to send out signals a couple of weeks ago that she might be similarly inclined. Unfortunately, she wasn't on duty. He stayed for dinner anyway, drank more than he intended, drove home erratically and tumbled into bed before eleven.

Some celebration.

FOUR

Webber had said nothing on the phone about how he was going to get the money to James. Presumably it would be by messenger, so James stayed close to the house all day. He didn't even go for a run on the beach, choosing to do a little work around the outside of the main house instead. Today there were no complaints from his tenant hanging over this head. No doubt Landers would come up with something pretty soon, but until he did, James was free to fix the lock on the outside door that led directly to the basement, nail back a couple of slats from the fence that separated his garden from the one next door, water the patch of grass between the guest and the main house and fix the screen on the kitchen door of the main house. It was a morning crammed with excitement.

The money arrived around lunchtime. James was just heading back towards the guest house to get himself something to eat when the front gate opened and Bill, of Gary and Bill fame, came through. At least James assumed it was Bill. His face was heavily bandaged. The parts of it not covered with bandages and sticking plaster were blue going on black. There were no greetings, no "nice to see you again, how have you been?"

"We've got some business to take care of," said Bill. He had trouble enunciating the words through lips that resembled a couple of pieces of raw liver. His top front teeth were gone and the ones at the bottom were broken in half. Still, any dentist would be able to fix him up for twelve or fifteen thousand dollars.

"Come on in," said James. He stood aside for Bill to precede him into the guesthouse. He didn't want this wounded butterfly anyplace other than where he could see him at all times. Bill would have had his instructions, money for the key, a simple exchange. But James didn't want to take the chance that, once business was over, Bill might want to indulge in a little free enterprise revenge, above and beyond the call of duty, applied with a knife or an iron piece.

"They sew your ear back on?" asked James. No point in not being polite.

"They tried. It didn't take."

James relaxed slightly. He'd been right, Bill was a pro and pros didn't bear long time grudges. They'd gone a couple of rounds together and James came out on top. They'd never be bosom buddies but business was business. On to the next deal.

"Is Gary still in the hospital?"

"He'll be flat on his back for a couple more weeks and walking with a limp for the rest of his life."

"That bad?"

"You broke his leg, remember?"

"Legs mend."

"They do if they're set right the first time."

"You went to a quack."

"You said 'don't go to UCLA.' Which was a pity because that's where he wound up. Trouble was, by the time we got there, his foot was pointing backwards."

"I'll send him some candy."

"Shove it up your ass. Where's the key?"

"Where's the money?"

Bill produced an envelope from the pocket of his jeans. James reached to take it but Bill held it back.

"The key." James handed him the key the hardware store had made up for him. Bill didn't even look at it. He stuffed it in his pocket and handed James the envelope. "Count it."

James checked the contents of the envelope. There were fifty, one hundred dollar bills. "Tell Mr. Webber it was a pleasure doing business with him."

"Go fuck yourself" said Bill, but without much animosity. He started for the door.

"What happens now?" James asked. "I figure Mr. Webber's pretty mad at the police for losing Menzies."

"What do you care? He's not worried. The kid will be taken care of, guaranteed." A moment later he was gone.

James counted the money again. He'd nearly been beat up by a couple of psychotic fags and he's been accused of a murder, but five grand was five grand. The bedroom would be redecorated and he'd have a couple of grand left over. Altogether, it had worked out fine for everybody except for Megan McCoy who was dead, and for Paul Menzies, who was likely going to nailed for it. Things had worked out especially well for whoever it was who had actually done the killing. In spite of Bill's veiled innuendo, it looked like he or she was going to get away with it. James would dearly have liked to know who the killer was. On the other hand, he also knew, as he locked away the money in his desk drawer, he wasn't going to lose any sleep over it.

His new carpet arrived a couple of days later, by which time he had repainted the bedroom. According to the newspapers and TV, the police were making progress in the Beverly Hills hotel killing and were expecting to charge somebody with the murder in a matter of hours. This meant they were getting no place fast which, in turn, meant that Paul had managed to slip out from under, at least for the time being. Landers found nothing more to complain about, instead he'd taken to hanging around the small garden that separated the main house from the guest house where he could keep an eye on the coming and goings to James' guest house, waiting for the next orgy to start.

Micklehaus called James on the third day. For somebody who was making no progress, he sounded remarkably cheerful. "How you doing, Reed?"

James was immediately suspicious. "Okay, Lieutenant. Yourself?"

"I was wondering if you've remembered anything you forgot to tell us before."

"I'd have told you if there was," said James.

"Sure, you would. Like you told us about Menzies."

"It slipped my mind."

"Yeah, well you don't have to worry about it anymore 'cause we've found him."

It figured, thought James. He felt a surge of sympathy for Paul. He hadn't even made it out of the state. "When?"

"This morning around six. We haven't officially identified the body yet, we figured you could do that for us."

"Why me?" said James, feeling slightly sick.

"You're the only person we know of who knows what the guy looks like."

"What happened?"

"We dropped the stake out on that tennis club. Looks like he went back. Maybe he decided to sack out. Anyway, there was a fire up that canyon last night."

James vaguely remembered it being reported on the early morning news: a small brush fire, very little structural damage, no casualties.

"I heard about it. Nobody said anything about casualties."

"Yeah, well, I guess they didn't know when they filed the story. The way I figure it, he was either too drunk or too stoned to run. Maybe he didn't even wake up. He was burned to a crisp."

"You sure it's Menzies?"

"Officially, if I was sure, I wouldn't be asking you to identify the body," said Micklehaus. "But yeah, I'm sure. His stuff is all over."

"What stuff?"

"Personal shit. It was in the back of the car out in the lot. Looked like he was getting ready to leave town."

"He didn't own a car."

"He rented it. We checked it out. So, you gonna identify him, or aren't you?

There was no way he could get out of it. "Where and when?"

"Downtown. The police morgue. Try to make it sometime today."

"Are you going to be there?"

"There's no need."

"Not even to gloat, lieutenant?"

"Hey Reed, here's a thought to carry around with you to comfort you in your old age. If you hadn't held out on us, we'd have got on to Menzies earlier and he likely wouldn't be dead now." Micklehaus hung up.

"Fuck you, too, Lieutenant," said James into the empty phone.

The guy on duty at the morgue was a cheerful young man, extremely happy in his line of work. His plastic name tag identified him as Alvin Weeks. He was expecting James, although Alvin didn't know what good it was going to do, because the dead guy's own mother wouldn't be able to recognize the burned corpse James had been asked to identify.

"It's a pure waste of time," Alvin said.

"That suits me fine," said James, preparing to leave.

"Wait. Orders are orders, and I've got mine. All you got to do is take a look. I'll ask you whether you identify the crisp as Paul Menzies. When you've finished throwing up, you nod your head. That way the Beverly Hills cops can put their paper work in order, the poor stiff gets himself buried, and everyone is happy, okay?"

"Okay," said James.

He followed Alvin along a bleak white corridor, the only sound the hum of the air conditioner and the squeak of rubber soled shoes.

"If the body's such a mess, how'd they figure it was Menzies in the first place?" James asked.

"Location, personal effects, prints, dental records."

"Wishful thinking?"

"It's been known."

It wasn't as bad as James had expected. The thing that occupied one of the drawers in the morgue bore so little resemblance to anything that had ever been human that James's stomach didn't even heave. It looked like a newly unwrapped Egyptian mummy. It was shriveled, drawn into a fetal attitude, the whole thing an even black color with a hint of charred bone showing here and there.

"Do you identify the body as that of Paul Menzies" said Alvin.

"Menzies was six feet two," said James. "He was built like a brick shit house."

"Lot of the fat and tissue just gets burned right away. Sylvester Stallone would look like this if he was in that kind of fire."

James looked again. What the hell did he know? Come to think of it, what the hell did he care?

"Could be him," he said.

"I need more than that."

"Very likely?"

"Not good enough."

James looked again, harder this time. "He's had a smack in the mouth."

"That's the least of his problems," said Alvin. He checked something on a clip board attached to the drawer. "It says here he was found under a drink vending machine. Looks like it fell on his face."

It still didn't look like Paul, but Bill had said Paul would be taken care of, so it was very unlikely to be anybody else.

"Will you settle for a highly probable?" asked James.

"Just nod your head, that's all I need," said Alvin.

James nodded his head.

He detoured on the way home and drove to the tennis club. There was a fire department notice at the entrance forbidding entry to anyone who wasn't authorized. Apart from that, there was no sign that anything had happened. But past the entrance, it was different. There were a couple of fire department vehicles in the parking lot, half-a-dozen firemen were spread out, moving slowly across the hills surrounding the club, checking for any remaining hot spots. The place still smelled of smoke. It was a depressing smell, only too familiar to Southern California canyon dwellers. What had been the club house was just a blackened heap of rubble with the skeleton of the drink vending machine, sticking out of the heap of ash like some *avant garde* piece of sculpture. James parked his car close to one of the fire department vehicles. Behind the wheel, a guy was sleeping with his visored cap pulled down over his face. James leaned in the window, "Hey, buddy."

The guy woke up with a start. A moment to orientate himself before looking pissed off at being awakened.

"Didn't you see the sign?"

"What sign?"

"We put a sign out on the highway, nobody allowed down here until we're through."

"No sign. What happened here?"

"For Christ's sake? What do you think happened? A fire happened."

"How'd it start?"

"Listen mister, either you got legitimate business here or you don't."

"I work for the insurance company," said James. "How'd the fire start?"

"What difference does it make?"

"We've gotta know before we pay out any claims."

"Man, you insurance people are all the same. You'll find any way so's you don't have to pay out the money. The fire started in or up over the hill."

"It couldn't have been the other way around?"

"See how the main part of the burned area fans out as it goes uphill? It spreads. If the fire had come down the hill, it would be the other way around. Is that what you wanted to hear?"

"Not particularly" said James. "What started it?"

"I dunno, maybe the stiff started it. Did they tell you there was a stiff?"

"They told me."

"He could have been having a barbecue, lighting a joint, letting off firework … you name it."

"I'm asking you to name it."

"What do I know? I drive a fire truck."

"Mind if I take a look?"

"Do whatever you like mister, just so long as you pay the guy his money."

James walked between the tennis courts to the charred mess of blackened timber and ash that used to be Paul's club house High on the hill above, one of the firemen called down to the guy in the truck that he'd found a hot spot. Either the guy didn't hear him or didn't think it was important enough to bother with because he stayed where he was, behind the wheel of his truck. In the center of what remained of the club house, there was an area where the floor boards were barely scorched, showing that the vending machine had fallen face down, effectively protecting the section of the floor from excessive heat and flame. Later, it had been lifted onto its side, no doubt to drag what remained of Paul out from under. The smell of burned wood was very strong. James thought that maybe there was another smell, cooked meat, but then it might just have been his imagination.

James walked back to the guy in the fire truck, who had just closed his eyes again and wasn't pleased to see him. "Okay, what now?"

"They found a hot spot on the hill back there," said James.

"I heard him."

"But aren't you supposed to do something about it?"

"What should we do? There's nothing left to burn."

He was right. The grass, the brush, everything flammable had long gone.

"How come the vending machine fell over?"

"Jesus, man, I don't know."

"Could there have been an explosion?"

"There could if there was any combustibles lying around."

"Like what?"

"Bottled gas, barbecue fluid, cleaning solvent, paint."

"Did you find any?"

The guy narrowed his already beady eyes. "I know what you're after. You figure if you can prove there was something flammable stored here then you won't have to pay out. Well fuck you, mister insurance man, I ain't saying no more." To emphasize his point, he wound up the window of his vehicle, pulled his hat back down over his eyes and pretended to go to sleep gain. James took one more look towards the tennis club. Two of the firemen at the edge of the hill were laughing at something one of them had said. Already the cicadas were beginning to move back in. A small bird of prey swooped down over the burned grassland looking for fried snake or roast field mouse, anything that might not have outrun the fire. Paul Menzies hadn't outrun the fire. James climbed back in his car and headed towards home.

❧   ❧   ❧

He emerged onto Pacific Coast Highway at Pepperdine University. The campus positively gleamed with its new white buildings, fresh green grass, and a scattering of handsome, healthy kids going about the business of growing up.

As he put the car in the garage, he kept his fingers crossed that he'd make it indoors without bumping into Landers. He was in no mood to play games right now. One word of complaint from his tenant and he'd be out on the street along with his wife, the maid and all their luggage and to hell with the rent. In fact, to hell with everything.

Maybe Landers felt the vibes because he didn't appear as James let himself into the guest house. He poured himself a large snort of the brandy that he kept for special occasions. Because this was indeed a special occasion. Requiem for a murdered youth. He raised the glass briefly.

"Mud in your eye, you poor, dumb son of a bitch."

He downed the drink and poured another. He drank this one more slowly and considered the life and times of the late Paul Menzies. A nice young man, ingenuous to the point of simplicity, and generous with himself, especially where the ladies were considered. That had been his main problem, winding up as Megan McCoy's boy toy. Then he decided Paul decided he'd had enough of her middle aged (from his point of view) hang ups, all that shit about wanting to get married. Who needs it! So packed his duffle bag and headed west, like a lot of young men before him. He was going to make it on his own in the land of milk and honey, where the sun never stops shining and everybody gets to be a movie star. All he got was dead. Too drunk or too stoned to get out from under a vending machine, according to Micklehaus.

But there was one problem with that assumption. Micklehaus didn't know that Paul didn't drink and didn't do drugs. His body was all he had going for him and he didn't mess around with it. On the other hand, maybe Micklehaus knew, but didn't care, because now he could close the book on the Megan McCoy killing.

So how did it happen?

Maybe someone spiked Paul's orange juice or whacked him over the head, then they tipped the vending machine onto his face before torching the place.

James poured another drink. Why knock over the vending machine on him? Paul had to have been either dead or unconscious before the fire was set, so what was the point? Unless he wasn't dead or unconscious.

Maybe Micklehaus had been right in one aspect of this theory. Paul had been sleeping in the club house, his attacker snuck in and pushed the vending machine on top of him. That was guaranteed to keep anybody quiet while they burned.

James decided it was as good a scenario as he was going to come up with right now, and who the hell cared anyway? He'd wanted out of the whole mess, and that's what he was.

Let's drink to being out of it. He raised his glass again. Shit, it was empty already.

He refilled it.

Not only was he out of it, he was five grand richer, courtesy of Mr. Jackson Megabucks Webber, sitting up there in his silk-lined, Fifth Avenue penthouse. Webber had wanted Paul taken are of and had seen to it that it was done.

James wondered briefly how much Webber had paid Bill. Perhaps Webber kept the two guys on a retainer to do all of his dirty work.

He poured himself another measure of his "special occasion brandy." It went down like velvet. He decided there should be more special occasions in his life. He was willing to bet Jackson Webber's life was one big special occasion, morning to night, day in, day out, month after month, just one great big party from January through December.

Okay…so let's be a party pooper. Let's show Mr. Jackson Sonofabitch Webber that life ain't necessarily always a bed of roses, especially when you stick it to a friend of James Reed, all around nice guy, at least ninety nine percent of the time, but a mean mother when he gets his dander up. And right now, his dander was up as high as four, or was it five, glasses of special occasion brandy could get it, which was pretty goddamn high considering it was only the middle of the afternoon and he hadn't had any lunch and right now he was working himself into as foul and vindictive a mood as he could remember having been in since God knew how long and by Christ he was going to do something about it pretty damn quick because what happened to Paul Menzies his good old buddy shouldn't happen to a dog and he was gonna do something about it the sooner the better or his name wasn't James Reed.

Right after a nap.

When he awoke his bedside clock said six thirty. Outside, it was either getting dark or getting light. It took him a few minutes to work out which. Eventually, he decided it was getting dark. He'd slept the afternoon away. He'd also slept away the effect of his "special occasion" brandy, leaving only the dregs. He felt murderous. Maybe a run on the beach would help. Then he decided the hell with it, he'd go the black coffee route.

He was into this third cup when Landers knocked on the door and opened it before James could tell him to fuck off. A quick look around showed Landers that there were no naked children, gay men, or wild animals debasing themselves, and he stepped inside.

"Mind if I come in?" he said, closing the door behind him.

"I'll fix it tomorrow," said James.

"I already fixed it," said Landers.

"So if nothing needs fixing, what do you want?"

"I've been talking to Abe on the phone this afternoon," said Landers, and when he got no reaction from James, he added: "Lock and key business Abe, I told you about him."

"Ah! Abe."

"Abe, I said, if I showed you a key to a locker, one of those Grand Central, Penn Station type lockers, how long's it gonna take you to find the locker it fits? You know what he told me?"

"What did he tell you, Mr. Landers?"

"He told me that providing the locker was someplace in New York, he'd have it pinpointed in forty-eight hours flat."

They call it the red eye because that's what you get flying coast-to-coast in the middle of the night. You take off from Los Angeles at midnight and you arrive in New York five hours later. At eight a.m. New York time. Everybody's day is just beginning. For the traveler from the west coast, it feels like the middle of the night. It had taken James exactly four hours to organize himself for the trip.

First, he had to talk himself into taking it, which he'd done within ten minutes of Landers leaving the guest house. He was pissed off at the idea that Webber was going to get away with ordering the murders of Megan McCoy and Paul Menzies So, big deal. People got away with murder all the time. Then James tried to look at things from Webber's point of view.

Here I am, thinks Webber, hugely rich, hugely respectable, and I've just gotten away with murder, except out there in La La Land there's a guy called James Reed who knows all about my involvement with Megan McCoy and Paul Menzies and those two crazy hoods who work for me and maybe it wouldn't be a bad idea if I took him out of the picture, especially since the key I've just paid James Reed five grand for doesn't open shit, which I

JIMMY SANGSTER

don't know yet, but which I'm probably going to find out one day which will mean that James Reed still has the real key, which is even better reason to do something about him.

To James, this whole line of thought seemed eminently reasonable. He would have thought along the same lines himself. He called American Airlines and booked himself on the red eye in four hours. Then he went over to the main house and rang the bell. The front door was opened by Carmelita, half black, half Hispanic and all bad temper.

"What y'all want?" she snarled.

"I want to talk to Mr. Landers."

"He's eating." She started to close the door. James put his hand flat on it and for a brief moment, the two of them pushed against each other like they were engaged in a personal conflict.

This is ridiculous, thought James. "Just tell him I want to talk to him, please." Must keep his British cool when dealing with domestic staff.

"I done told you, he's eatin. Come back later."

Okay, he decided, forget the cool. "Tell him now, you bloody old harridan or I'll have you all out of my house before you can say Jesse Jackson."

She looked at him for a long moment. Then she stepped back from the front door. "Why don' y'all come on in. I'll tell him." She even gave him something which could have been a grin before shuffling off in the direction of the dining room.

Landers appeared a couple of seconds later, wiping his mouth on a napkin. James apologized for interrupting dinner. He told Landers he was leaving for New York in a couple of hours and could Landers call his friend Abe and let him know James was coming to town and would be grateful for any help Abe could give him?

"What should I do if something goes wrong here in the house and the landlord's in New York?" asked Landers.

"I'll be back in a few days. A week at the most."

"The roof could blow off and the place burn down in a week."

"So, I'll refund part of your rent," said James.

Landers promised to call Abe Schiner first thing tomorrow.

"Can't you call him now?"

"It's already eleven p.m. in New York," said Landers. "I don't call my friends after nine."

James agreed he'd call Landers from New York as soon as he got in. Landers wished him *bon voyage* and went back to his dinner.

James went back to the guesthouse, threw some stuff into an overnight bag, checked that he had his credit cards, and drove to the airport. There, he parked his car in a prominent slot in the long-term parking lot. He didn't lock it. Maybe one day he'd get lucky and somebody would steal it. He picked up and paid for his ticket, grabbed something to eat in the coffee shop, had a couple of stiff belts in the bar before boarding the flight with the other passengers, most of whom looked as miserable as he felt. He strapped himself into a window seat in the nonsmoking section. A large man with strong body odor sat next to him. Fortunately, immediately after takeoff, the large man commandeered four empty seats in the middle of the aircraft and sacked out. This left James with three seats to himself. He, too, tried to sack out but try as he might, he couldn't avoid one of other of his feet sticking into the gangway, where it got banged every time anybody went up or down to the john or the galley. In the end, he gave up trying to sleep horizontally. He tried watching the movie for a time, but that gave him a headache. Finally, forty-five minutes out of New York, he managed to fall asleep. When the stewardess woke him and hold him to fasten his seat belt, it was like being dragged back from the dead.

He staggered through the arrivals terminal like he was sleep walking through a particularly bad nightmare. Nothing seemed quite real. The light was too bright, the air conditioning in the terminal building too cold, the noise level too high, the people too pushy. The blast of hot, damp air when he finally collected his bag and moved outside was like peering around the doorway into a particularly wet version of hell. Outside the terminal, he grabbed the first cab he could find and told the driver to take him to the Gramercy Park Hotel. The driver didn't speak English and didn't know where it was, but he did have a map of Manhattan on which James pointed out his destination. He half expected the driver to tell him he wasn't sure where Manhattan was either.

James had stayed at the Gramercy Park Hotel before. He didn't like it much. But there was very little about New York that he did like. They didn't have a room at the hotel, but Mr. Reed was in luck because they did have a suite overlooking Gramercy Park, which he could have providing he agreed to vacate by the weekend. James didn't want a suite, and he had no idea whether or not he'd be through by the weekend. But he wanted a shower and a couple hours sleep and he wanted it right now. So, he said he'd take the suite.

"It's two twenty-five a day, sir," said the clerk. "Plus tax."

James was too tired to negotiate. "I'll take it."

The clerk examined the credit card closely. Then he conferred with a colleague before asking James if he could see his passport.

"This is New York, for Christ's sake," said James, who was not feeling very chipper.

"I'm sorry sir, I thought you were English. Your accent."

"I am. I was. What's that got to do with it?"

"We need an ID, sir."

James produced his driver's license, which the clerk examined with the same air of suspicion as he had the credit card.

"I'm not looking to buy the hotel," said James, patience just about exhausted. "Just rent a room."

Another conference with a colleague, a quick call to the credit card company just to make sure the card hadn't been stolen and the clerk decided to take a chance. He allowed James to register. He directed him towards an elevator at the back of the lobby, through a small public area where all the armchairs were occupied by the exhausted members of a Japanese tour group trying to grab forty winks between an early breakfast and the top of the Empire State Building. When James finally reached his room and saw himself in the mirror, he understood the desk clerk's hesitation. He was unshaven, and he still had traces of the bruise left by Bill's iron pipe, his eyes were red rimmed from lack of sleep and red lined from yesterday's one-man wake, all this wrapped in the general untidiness that resulted from sitting on an airplane all night. He looked like an unsuccessful bum. He decided that he didn't smell too good either.

He rang down for some orange juice and coffee, stripped off all his clothes and took a shower. He drank his juice and coffee, hung out the DO NOT DISTURB sign and hit the sack. He woke up four hours later without the remotest idea where he was. Outside, he could hear the steady noise of traffic overlaid with distant sirens. It was that sound that finally orientated him. It was one of the constants in Manhattan. He climbed out of bed and looked out the window. Ten floors down was the small patch of green that was Gramercy Park, hemmed in on all four sides by old, rather dignified buildings which had obviously seen better days. He opened the sash window and was engulfed in a wave of hot, damp air overlaid with exhaust fumes. Two dirty pigeons, resting on the ledge just outside his window couldn't even pluck up the energy to fly off. They both stared at James, beady eyed, just daring him to make a move towards them. He closed the window quickly allowing the air conditioner to take over once more before going through to the bathroom and taking another shower. Then he called Landers.

"Did you talk to Abe yet?"

"I talked to him. I told him you'd call him." Landers gave him a number in Manhattan. "That's his private line."

James thanked him and was about to hang up when Landers told him he'd had a visitor first thing this morning. "I was out on the terrace when I heard this guy banging on your front door. So, like a good neighbor I go round to see who's making all the noise. The guy tells me he wants to see you real bad and I tell the guy you're in New York so he's gonna have to wait. Where in New York, he wants to know and I tell him I don't know but maybe if he got in touch with Abe Schiner, Abe would tell him. Man, he was an angry one. I thought for a minute there he was going to bang me over the head with one of his crutches."

"Did he tell you his name?"

"I didn't ask."

"About twenty-three; dark hair; well built?"

"That's him."

"Was his friend with him?" said James.

"Men like that don't have friends."

"Same age, fair, with a mouth full of smashed teeth and a face to match."

"My God, Reed. The people you know! No, sir. There was nobody like that. Did I do right? I mean, telling him you were in New York."

No point in giving Landers a hard time. "You did right, Mr. Landers. Thanks."

Still Landers didn't let him go. "If any of your young friends turn up looking for one of your parties, who do I tell them?"

"Tell them you're standing in for me," said James. "Have a nice day."

He hung up.

Okay, so Gary was out of the hospital and looking for him. What did he want and where was Bill? On reflection, who cared? They were there, and he was here, two and half thousand miles away. So maybe they could trace him through Abe, but as far a James was concerned, they had no more business together, so why bother? He called the number Landers had given him for Abe. It was picked up almost immediately.

"Schiner."

"My name is James Reed, Mr. Schiner. I believer Mr. Landers called about me?"

"Hey, sure, Bernie told me all about you. You're the sex deviant. Right?"

"That's me, Mr. Schiner."

"Call me Abe. What can I do for you?"

"Mr. Landers said you might be able to locate a public locker for me if I let you have the key."

"I can give it my best shot, Jim. Did Bernie tell you I was into stuff like that?"

"Locks and keys?"

"Kinky sex."

"It didn't come up."

"Like, I'm not into it yet, but I been thinking about getting into it. Maybe you can give me some advice when you schlep the key round."

"I'll do my best," said James. "Where are you located?"

"I got an office just off Madison on 75th." He gave James the number. "You can't miss it. My name is on the door."

James decided to walk to Schiner's office. He realized he'd made a mistake the moment he emerged from the hotel. It was the fifth straight day of a heatwave and before James had even reached 23rd Street, a block and half from the hotel, he was soaking wet. He tried to find a cab, without luck, so he caught a bus. It would have been more convenient to take the subway, but if his memory served him right from the last time he'd taken it, it wasn't air conditioned, it smelled of stale piss, was knee deep in garbage, and somebody had thrown up on his shoes.

As it turned out, the bus wasn't much of an improvement. The air conditioner had broken down and as he fumbled for change the driver snarled at him as if he was personally responsible for the malfunction. His fellow passengers were all into hate thy neighbor, their expressions saying: "Don't look sideways at me buddy, or I'll break your face." There was a monumental traffic jam on Madison, starting around 44th Street. After fifteen sweaty minutes, during which the bus hadn't moved a yard, James asked the driver to open he door so he cold get out and walk. The driver refused, using as an excuse that he was forbidden by the rules from opening the doors except at a bus stop or in an emergency.

"This is an emergency," said James.

"What emergency?" snarled the driver.

"Bus driver beaten up by irate passenger," said James.

The driver thought about the threat. He was a big guy, with an ugly, bully boy face. For a moment, James thought he might have pushed his luck a fraction too far. But the driver was out of condition and anyway, it was too hot. He opened the doors. James got out fast before the driver could slam them on his heels. Almost immediately the traffic jam started to break up and James was treated to the sight of the bus overtaking him. The driver gave him the finger while the passengers leered down at him, each one happy to be rid of the asshole.

James stayed on Madison as far as 59th Street before cutting across a block to 5th Avenue. At least this way he could walk beside Central park, even kid himself the view of the trees made it cooler. At 75th Street, he turned right and started to look for the number Schiner had given him. It was on the other side of Madison, across from the Whitney Museum. The last time, the only time, he'd been to the Whitney was to a black-tie affair with Katherine. They'd been staying at the Plaza and they'd been picked up by a limo and flash bulbs had popped like starbursts as they arrived. It was a long time ago. Nowadays he didn't even own a black tie.

James was looking for a locksmith or an upmarket hardware store. For a moment, he thought Schiner had given him the wrong street number. He was outside a dignified old house. Then he saw Schiner's name on the door, as promised. A brass plaque with SCHINER engraved in fine copperplate, the whole thing polished almost out of existence. He climbed the four broad steps to the front door and rang the single bell. A moment later a disembodied voice asked him to face to his right, state his name and his business. He turned towards a small security camera that he hadn't spotted before.

"James Reed to see Abe Schiner."

After a few seconds, there was the sound of locks being disengaged and the front door opened automatically at the same time as the voice asked him to step inside.

The lobby was cool and magnificent. The place looked as it probably had a hundred years ago when it was occupied by whatever multi-millionaire robber baron had built it. The one concession to commerce was the uniformed man seated behind a Louis XV desk to the left of the front door, fronted by half a dozen small TV monitors. He was crew cut and built like a brick shit house. As James came in, the front door closed behind him with a solid clunk.

"Sign the book, sir," said the Brick Shit House behind the desk.

"It doesn't matter Horatio," a woman's voice said. "I'll take care of Mr. Reed."

The woman was standing at the top of the impressive flight of stairs leading up from the hall. She was about thirty-nine years old, dressed in a severely cut dark suit over a silk shirt. She looked like she'd spent the last five hours at the beauty parlor or hairdresser or both. James couldn't remember when he'd last seen anybody so immaculately put together.

"He's got to sign the book, Ms. Francis," said Horatio, the brick shit house. "Rules are rules."

James could hear her sigh from where he stood. "Would you mind, Mr. Reed?"

He walked over to the desk and signed his name in the book that Horatio pashed across to him.

"Gotta stick to the rules," said James.

"Right," said Horatio, slashing a venomous look towards Mr. Francis at the top of the stairs.

As James mounted the stairs, he caught a whiff of her perfume. Whatever it was, he decided, it shouldn't be allowed, not unless the wearer was prepared to have her bones jumped more of less on an hourly basis. She had dark hair, blue eyes, a generous mouth and magnificent teeth, which she now flashed at James as he reached the top of the stairs.

"I'm Wanda Francis, Mr. Schiner's personal assistant. He'll see you right away."

There was a trace of an accent in her voice that James couldn't place. He followed her along a paneled corridor towards double doors at the far end. There were some interesting looking paintings hanging on the walls which he would liked to have looked at, but his attention was elsewhere. Ms. Francis's suit wasn't as severely cut as he'd first thought. There was a lot of room for movement under her skirt which was just as well because here was a lot of movement taking place. It was extremely voluptuous, made even more so by the fact that James would have taken money she wasn't aware of the effect she was having on him. Ms. Francis. That didn't tell him a thing. They all call themselves Ms. these days. He caught up with her, mainly to see if she was wearing a wedding band, which she wasn't, but also to catch another whiff of her perfume. And having drawn alongside, he had to make some kind of conversation.

"The lock and key business must be booming."

"You must have been talking to Mr. Landers."

"Right."

"He's the one who calls it Mr. Schiner's lock and key business. I suppose it is in a way. It S.S.S."

James had heard of S.S.S. It was a multimillion-dollar corporation, one of the largest private security companies in the country, into everything from armored cars to bodyguards, from burglar alarm systems to, of course, locks and keys. At one time, when divorce between himself and Katherine had first loomed, he'd even considered applying to them for some kind of a job. After all, that's what he'd been doing when he'd met Katherine and become a distaff member of the celebrity circuit. Then, when Katherine had given him the beach house as a divorce settlement, he'd decided he didn't need a job after all.

"Let me guess," said James. "Schiner's Security Systems."

Ms. Francis flashed her magnificent teeth. "Go to the top of the class," she said.

"Will the teacher be there?" He wasn't going to be in New York long. Certainly not long enough to beat around too many bushes.

She looked at him steadily for a moment, weighing him up. Maybe she decided California scruffy would make a pleasant change of pace in bed.

"That's a distinct possibility," she said.

Woo-wee.

Abe Schiner was small, round and bald. He leapt up from behind a huge desk as Wanda Francis showed James into his office.

"Come in Jim. Is it okay if I call you Jim? You can call me Abe. Sit down. It's nice to see you. How are you enjoying New York? You want a cup of coffee? A drink? Give the man what he wants Wanda."

Abe was one highly-caffeinated guy.

"What would you like Mr. Reed?" asked Wanda Francis.

"Right now, I'll settle for a drink," said James. "Scotch and water."

She fetched him his drink from a bar concealed behind the bookcase and then glided out of the office.

"So, Jim, what can I do for you?" asked Abe Schiner.

James gave him the locker key. "Find the locker this belongs to."

Abe looked at the key, turning it over a couple of times. Then he pressed a button on his desk. A moment later, the door opened and Wanda Francis came back in.

Abe handed her the key. "Give this to Ted. Tell him I want to know where it belongs ASAP. Then stay in touch with Mr. Reed here. Let him know how we're getting on. All right?"

She flashed a quick glance at James. "Perfectly," she said.

As soon as she'd left the office again, Abe got down to important matters. "So listen, Jim. You got any contacts here in New York?"

"What kind of contacts?" asked James, knowing perfectly well what Abe was aluding to.

"You know. Stuff like Bernie's been telling me about you."

"Sex stuff?"

"Right. Sex stuff."

"I've got to be honest with you, Abe. The sex scene isn't what it was. No sir. First off, there's a good chance you're gonna get arrested."

"For screwing?"

"For underage screwing. That's what you're interested in, isn't it?" James pointed at a framed photograph on Abe's desk of two rather plain-looking girls, aged fourteen or thereabouts. "Young meat like those two."

"They're my granddaughters for God's sake," said Abe.

"They're all somebody's granddaughter, Abe."

Abe thought about it for a moment. "I was thinking of maybe a bit older."

"Fair enough," said James. "Trouble there is you've got a better than fifty percent chance of catching something."

"Like what?"

"You name it, Abe. Chances are they've got it."

"Social diseases? Clap? Stuff like that?"

"AIDs even."

Abe was silent. Time to move in for the kill. "What's your primary interest, Abe. Boys or girls?"

"Jesus Christ!" Abe was truly horrified. "What do you take me for?"

"A pervert, Abe. That's what we are talking about isn't it?"

Abe thought about it a moment. "I guess we are," he said. "Still, we're only talking about it. Right?"

"So far."

"So, listen. You keep in touch with Wanda out there. She'll let you know how things are coming along. Ted's a good man. Been working for me since I started the business forty years ago. Talk to him if you like. There's nothing he don't know about locks and keys. He should have some news for you in couple of days at most. How does that sound?"

"Just great. And you don't want me to fix you up with anything while I'm in town?"

"Next time maybe. And listen, Jim do me a favor. Don't mention this little talk we had to anyone. Okay?"

"Whatever you say, Abe."

"Anything else I can do for you while you're in town?"

To his vast relief, James told him there wasn't.

Wanda had an office adjoining Abe's.

"Your boss says I should talk to Ted," said James.

"Third door along the passage," said Wanda.

"He also says you and I should keep in touch."

"Sounds like it could be fun."

"Starting with lunch?"

"It's two thirty. I've already eaten."

"What time do you get hungry again?"

"Around seven thirty."

"Where around seven thirty?"

"Park Towers West on 66th Street, Apartment 1407. And bring lots of money, I've got very esoteric eating habits."

"So have I," said James.

"So, what's in this locker that's so important?"

"I won't know until I find out," said James. He gave her the number of the Gramercy Park Hotel, in case Ted the locksmith needed to reach him. "Incidentally, if anyone calls wanting to know where I'm at, I'd prefer you kept it to yourself."

She looked at him speculatively for a moment. "You're turning out to be a bit of a mystery figure," she said. "Maybe it's not such a good idea us having dinner."

"I think it's an excellent idea," said James. "See you at seven thirty."

Downstairs, Horatio asked him sign out. "Rules. Right?" said James.

"Right," said Horatio. James signed the book and Horatio hit a switch. The front door opened automatically.

"Very impressive," said James.

"It's crap, but the customers like it," said Horatio.

He was feeling a little better. Not much, but sufficient to consider walking the fifty odd blocks back to the hotel. Besides he wanted to take a look at Webber's High Tower.

It was a sixty-story building of steel and glass, not as quite as vulgar as Trump Tower. James walked in through the main entrance on Fifty into an atrium type lobby, which, unlike Trump's, contained no shops or restaurants, just jungle. A bank of elevators lined both sides of the atrium, which went up five stories narrowing as it got higher. Projections from the walls, at varying heights, provided places where foliage had been planted, everything from shrubbery to what appeared to James like fair-sized trees. Standing in the center of the lobby, looking up through all that greenery and seeing no sky, was a bit like being in the Amazonian rain forest. The impression was heightened by the sounds of exotic birdsong. There wasn't a bird in sight, exotic or otherwise. James realized the sounds were being piped in. He thought the same applied to the sound of running water until he saw the waterfall against the back wall tumbling down over fake rocks into a small pool. He walked over to the pool and peered into the dark waters, half expecting a crocodile to emerge. A school of immensely fat gold fish trolled around complacently.

"Can I help you, sir?" A large, uniformed black guy, one of half-a-dozen scattered throughout the jungle had moved up behind him.

"Just looking," said James.

"Unless you have specific business here, sir, I'm afraid I must ask you to leave."

"No feeding the fish?"

The guy didn't crack a smile. "No, sir." His left hand moved almost imperceptibly, a signal to his compatriots that maybe they'd got a minor crazy to deal with here. A couple of them drifted over.

"Next time you see Jackson Webber, tell him James Reed was asking after him," said James. He turned and headed for the main entrance.

"Excuse me, sir." The black guy caught up with him. "You wish to leave a message for Mr. Webber?"

"I just did," said James.

On his way back to the hotel, James stopped into a men's store and bought himself a new shirt. He was about to buy a necktie to go with it when he decided against it. If he turned up for his date wearing a tie, there was no telling how far upmarket Ms. Wanda Francis' choice of restaurant might reach, Lutèce or Brussels or some other $250-per-couple joint. There were plenty of them, places where a tie was mandatory. At least, that's how it had been when he was last here. But in those days, he was escorting his wife, Katherine Long, superstar and it didn't matter whether he wore a tie or not, nobody ever took any notice of him anyway.

Next to the men's store was a deli, which reminded him that the last food he'd seen had been on the airplane. Being airplane food, he hadn't eaten it. Right now, he was starving. He went in and sat at a table by the window where he could watch the passing parade.

A tired-looking, middle aged waitress dropped a menu in front of him and stood, pencil poised, "Whaddya want?"

James ordered a large pastrami sandwich.

"Large, extra-large or super large?"

"Super," said James.

"With everything?"

"The lot."

"You got it, mister."

In fact, it was five minutes before he got it. The sandwich that arrived resembled a two-story building and was accompanied by coleslaw, pickles and french fries, all-in-all enough food to choke a horse. He washed it down with a beer and left the deli twenty-five minutes later feeling like he'd never need to eat again.

Bored now with walking, he took a chance and climbed aboard a bus, traveling down Fifth Avenue. The air conditioning was working and the driver didn't snarl at any of his passengers. Burping contentedly, James felt relaxed for the first time since he had landed in New York. He'd done everything he could for the time being. All that remained now was for Ted to come up with the information on the locker that Megan McCoy had used. Maybe then he'd know exactly what it was that Webber had been prepared to kill for. Then would come the big decision. What to do with all this information. Still, that was in the future, in the meantime, he had a date with a sexy lady.

Maybe New York wasn't going to be as bad as he remembered after all.

FIVE

He left the hotel at 6:45. His date was for 7:30, but this was New York, where around this time in the evening nobody expected to find a cab. He picked one up only fifteen feet from the hotel, so he was dropped off outside the Lincoln Center half-an-hour before he was due to meet Wanda Francis. Some big function was going on at The Metropolitan Opera House. Limos were disgorging their passengers on Columbus Avenue, leaving them to walk in their finery across the plaza. James watched for a time. Maybe Mr. and Mrs. Jackson Webber were among the glittering couples. According to Paul Menzies, "him and his wife were always going to concerts and operas and things they do at the Lincoln Center." That's when he saw Katherine. She was on the arm of a distinguished looking, grey-haired man whom James vaguely recognized from the newspaper pictures as an up-and-coming politician. Katherine looked very good, indeed. But then she'd always blossomed in New York. The couple were surrounded by a small pack of hangers-on and photographers as they made their way towards the Opera House. They passed within a few feet of where James was standing, holding hands like lovers sometimes do. He had a momentary impulse to call her name and identify himself, maybe throw her off balance for a couple of seconds. But then they were past him, the focal point of a small flotilla of popping flashlights and admiring fans. Small world. James decided he'd try to identify the politician next time he saw his picture so's he'd remember not to vote for him. He wasn't quite sure why, but he hoped his ex-wife would not enjoy herself at the opera. And having formulated that thought, he felt like a shit for being so petty-minded.

He walked the couple of blocks to 66th Street, where he turned down past the Chinese embassy with its ever-present police guard mounted in a small shelter out on the sidewalk. The 24/7 police presence made this section of 66th, a very safe part of New York. A good location for a single lady to live. The apartment building, like it's neighbors, was tall and anonymous. There was a truculent doorman on duty, just inside the main entrance, who said he didn't think Ms. Francis was at home right now, but if James insisted, he'd try to reach her on the house phone, but he didn't think he'd have any luck because if she'd have come in, he'd have spotted her. At the same time he was making that speech, he managed to give the impression that if James felt like slipping him a dollar or two, then no doubt everything would be different and Ms. Francis would be at home just waiting for James's arrival. James kept his hands out of his pockets and told the guy to call the apartment. Wanda answered the phone right away and told the doorman to send James on up.

"Apartment 1507," said the porter.

"She told me fourteen," said James.

"Right, fourteen," said the porter. Shit, James wasn't gonna be any fun at all

He rang the door bell of 1407 and, because this was New York, he stood waiting while the inevitable bolts and deadlocks on the inside were taken care of. After a couple of minutes, and a considerable amount of noise, Wanda opened the door to him. It was exactly seven thirty, so he was a little surprised to find she was ready. The ladies he normally dated didn't expect you to turn up until at least fifteen minutes after the appointed time and then you were usually kept waiting another fifteen before she emerged from her toilette. James usually used that time to check her place out. He liked to think he could learn a lot about a woman from the way she furnished and decorated her apartment, the odd personal things she left lying around, photographs, books, magazines, and the paintings on the wall. But Wanda didn't give him time.

"I've made a reservation for eight," she said. "It's only five minutes from here so we've time to walk Prune first."

Prune turned out to be a small, jet black poodle with a stylish haircut and a bright pink ribbon in his hair. His toenails were painted the same pink as the ribbon and he wore a diamonte collar. If one overlooked these lapses, he turned out to be just another dog, sniffing and cocking his leg just like any old common garden mutt. He even had a personality which James found quite endearing when, as they brought him back into the building, he tried to bite the doorman who'd given James a hard time.

"That dog's gonna have to go, Ms. Francis," the doorman said to Wanda as she pulled Prune towards the elevators.

"Go fuck yourself, Ben," said Wanda, amicably.

Having deposited Prune back in the apartment, Wanda decided there was just time for a quick drink before going to the restaurant. James asked for a scotch.

"I've only got wine. Red or white?"

James asked for white, expecting a glass of Californian Chablis, which shouldn't happen to a dog. Instead, the wine she gave him was quite magnificent. He complimented her on it and she showed him the bottle. It was a Puligny-Montrachet '76.

"I'm into wines," she said.

At forty-five bucks a bottle, she must be into wine merchants too, unless Abe Schiner was paying her far more than he should. Still, none of this was any of James's business. All he was interested in was a pleasant dinner, some intelligent conversation, followed by a good solid roll in the sack at the end of the evening. His tastes like his ambitions, weren't extravagant.

Before they left for the restaurant James asked if he could use the bathroom. He needed to pee, certainly, but he also wanted to check out the medicine chest for signs of masculine occupation. If he'd found a shaving brush and razor, he'd have suggested an after-dinner drink back at his own hotel, rather than here in her apartment. But there was nothing like that. A bathroom smelling warm, moist and perfumed, cluttered with purely female accoutrements adjoining a very feminine bedroom with a companionable queen-sized bed.

When he came out of the bathroom, she was sitting at her vanity, retouching her makeup. She was wearing a silk shirt, tucked into a full, lightweight skirt. As she leaned forward to check in the mirror, the shirt gaped in the front and James saw that we wasn't wearing a bra. Her breasts were small, with very pronounced nipples. Suddenly he felt very horny. He realized that she was watching him in the mirror, an amused glint in her eye. For one desperate moment, he wondered how she would react if he suggested bed first, dinner afterwards. Then reason prevailed. He damped down his urges and went back into the living room. She joined him a couple of minutes later. They finished their wine. Prune was exhorted to "look after the apartment" and they left for dinner. On the way out, she double-locked the front door. Standing with her in the elevator, he was reminded how potent her perfume was.

"Nice perfume," he said.

"Thank you."

"Good taste."

"I'm glad," she said. "I wear it all over."

"Where are we eating?" asked James, trying to get the thickness out of his voice. He hoped it was going to be someplace where the service was reasonably efficient and they could get done and back to the apartment before he burst.

She took him to a restaurant between Columbus and Central Park on 72nd. It was Italian, pretentious, and hugely expensive.

She knew the *maître d'hotel* and half the clientele. Later in the meal, he discovered she also knew the chef/owner as he came out from the kitchen and did them the honor of sitting at their table while he consumed two large cognacs, which James later found had been put on his bill. The menu was heavy on the pastas and the wine list heavy on the prices.

"You're into wine," he said, handling her the *carte du vin*. "You choose."

He knew instinctively it was something he was going to regret. But she looked so pleased at being asked that he decided it had been a good move, whatever it was going to cost him.

"Do you prefer Italian or French?" she asked him.

"Seeing as we're eating Italian, let's drink it too," he said, in the knowledge that Italian wine was invariably cheaper than French.

She didn't even look at the wine list. "We'll have a bottle of Brunello di Montalcino '71."

The wine waiter was full of regretful apologies, they were out of the '71. If the *signorina* remembered, she drank the last bottle herself when she was here a couple of weeks ago. But there was still a bottle of '75 in the cellar.

Wanda told him the '75 would have to do. Meanwhile, she'd have a Cinzano Bianco and whatever James would like. He ordered a large scotch. The regular waiter took over from the wine waiter and recited the specialties of the day.

James was always wary of ordering something that wasn't on the menu. He'd been told once by a restaurant owner that the expensive items were often plugged verbally because there was no mention of the price as there was on the written menu, and most men were too embarrassed to ask what something was going to cost in front of their date. She surprised him by ordering a plate of the special house pasta for the both of them. She told the waiter that they'd decide on the main course while eating the pasta.

"It's a spaghetti with a seafood sauce," she told James. "I think you'll like it."

Pasta with fish sauce. Maybe he was going to get off lightly after all.

"So, tell me about James Reed from California," she said, as the waiter left them.

"What do you want to know?"

"Are you really a sex deviant?"

"You've been tapping your bosses telephone calls."

"I have to, or the business would collapse. He forgets ninety percent of what he says on the phone. But you're evading the question."

"What sexual behavior do you consider deviant?"

"Practically nothing," she said. "Providing it involves people who've reached the age of consent and it doesn't leave any scars."

James told her briefly about Landers' misconceptions, without going into too much detail.

"But you didn't give him an argument," she said.

"That would have spoiled his fun." He wanted to change the subject. "Okay. Your turn. Tell me about Wanda Francis."

She'd been married, divorced a couple of years. No kids. Ex-husband was something on Wall Street, and, according to her, a first-class asshole to boot. She liked being on her own. She didn't much like the New York, but this was where it was all happening. She was part owner with a girl friend of a small place in Connecticut, where where liked to go weekends. She liked her job, and Abe and, all in all, she was more or less satisfied with her lot.

The prima piatti arrived and the conversation ceased. The seafood mixed in with the pasta turned out to be caviar, and the dish cost thirty-five bucks apiece. But the entrée only set him back thirty bucks a plate, so he figured he was ahead, until the bill arrived and he discovered the wine had cost eighty bucks and, what with the patron's cognac, the desert, the coffee, the taxes and the tips, the total came to a shade over $350, and they didn't take credit cards.

"Tough," said James. "That's all I've got."

"A check would be acceptable," said the *maître d'hotel*, who had appeared from nowhere.

"It's an out-of-town check," said James.

"Perfectly acceptable, sir. Seeing you are a good friend of *la bella signorina* Francis."

At these prices, about to become an even better one, thought James as he wrote out his check.

They were bowed out of the restaurant like departing royalty. The doorman asked if they wanted a cab. Wanda said it was only six blocks, they'd walk. The gothic looking bulk of the Dakota loomed across from the restaurant.

"That's where John Lennon was murdered," said Wanda.

"I was there once," said James.

"The Dakota?"

"John Lennon's."

She was impressed. "You knew John Lennon?"

"I was with my ex-wife at the time. She knew everyone."

"Who's your ex-wife?"

James told her. Wanda was even more impressed. She tucked her arm under his, pressing closer to him as they walked. If he'd known her reaction would be, he could have dropped Katherine's name earlier and saved himself $350.

It was past eleven, but Columbia Avenue was busy with pedestrian traffic. Theatres and restaurants were emptying out, while bars were doing a roaring trade. There were even some stores still open, while the sidewalks at the junction with Broadway were like an African market place, cluttered with black street traders. There was a new doorman on duty at Wanda's apartment building. He didn't even wake up as they came in.

"I have to walk Prune," she said.

They collected an over-excited Prune and walked him up and down 66th, past the cop in the booth outside the Chinese embassy, who apparently knew Wanda and Prune from other nighttime walks. Wanda dutifully scooped the poop and eventually decided Prune had squeezed out everything he was going to.

"Feel like a nightcap?" she asked James.

"Just a quick one," he said.

Ten minutes later, he was in bed as she came out of the bathroom wearing nothing but a wide leather belt and high heel shoes.

"What's the belt for?" he said.

"Something for you to hang onto," she said as she climbed on top of him. "It's going to be a rough ride."

It was a long night. Far longer than James had believed himself capable of. After he'd gasped his way to a noisy orgasm, flattered that she'd stayed with him all the way, he was prepared to deliver the polite few minutes of tenderness before dropping off to sleep. She had other ideas. With judicious use of a finger or tongue or both, she managed to get him to rise to the occasion twice more before she finally let him go to sleep. But not for long. She awoke him around six a.m.

"Please, not again," he said.

"One for the road," she said.

"Who's leaving?"

"You are, in a few minutes."

"It's the middle of the night."

"It's six a.m. I want you out of here before the day shift comes on downstairs."

Whatever. She was the one who lived here. If she wanted to protect her, reputation she was entitled. James started to struggle out of bed. She dragged him back. "I told you. One for the road."

"If you can make it work, good luck," said James.

She disappeared into the bathroom for a moment and reappeared with a battery powered electric toothbrush.

"What are you going to do with that?" asked James.

"I'm not going to clean my teeth," said Wanda, climbing back into bed.

Fifteen minutes later, James ungritted his teeth and told her that whatever she'd been doing she should patent and sell to the electric toothbrush makers, their sales would quadruple overnight. And please, would she do it one more time.

"Party over," she said. "Don't slam the door on the way out."

James struggled out of bed and into his clothes. Prune, who'd been sleep on James's pants, which had been thrown onto the bedroom chair, now took his rightful place on the bed and, after one triumphant glare in James's direction, went back to sleep. James found a clothes brush and managed to get most of the black hair off his pants before pulling them on. He would have liked to have kissed Wanda goodbye, but he hadn't cleaned his teeth, and remembering where he'd been nuzzling around last night, he didn't figure his mouth would taste too inviting. He satisfied himself, blowing her a kiss from the bedroom door.

"I'll call you later," he said. But she had already gone back to sleep.

As he let himself out of the apartment, he caught sight of his reflection in the mirror behind the front door. He decided he looked well and truly fucking great in every sense of the word. Going down in the elevator, he tried to member the last time sex had been so good. By the time he reached the first floor, he had started to feel horny again. Wanda Francis was one very sexy lady. She was bright too, and amusing and intelligent. If he could break her of her restaurant habits, he might get to enjoy his stay in New York, maybe even get involved in a relationship which was more then a series of one-night stands. It had been a long, long time since anything like that had happened.

The night doorman was still on duty. He'd been asleep when James had arrived with Wanda, so he had no idea who this was, limping out of the place at the crack of dawn, looking like he'd spent the night standing up. For all he knew, James could be a burglar, a rapist or a mass murderer and, right now, everybody in the building could be dead with their throats slit. They didn't pay him enough money to deal with that kind of shit. James could see him trying to make up his mind whether to challenge him or not. He helped the guy come to his decision by glaring hard and looking mean. The doorman disappeared behind the desk, ostensibly look for something he'd temporarily mislaid. By the time he looked up again, James was out on the street.

Ted called him around quarter of twelve. James had gone straight to bed when he'd reached the hotel. Last night had been short on sleep time. The phone call dragged him back from the dead.

"You got lucky," said Ted after he had identified himself. "Then again maybe not so lucky."

"Tell me," said James.

"I've got four locker locations that your key will fit."

"Four ... what's with four?"

"I'll tell you about it when you get here. Say one thirty."

"One thirty will be fine," said James.

As he climbed out of bed, he heard the maid come into the sitting room of his suite. He grabbed the sheet round his nakedness just as she stuck her head into the bedroom.

"You're still here," she said, ignoring his condition.

"That's why I put the do not disturb sign on the door," said James.

"Honey, you had that sign on your door practically since you done checked in. What is it with you? You on night work, you got to be sleeping all day?"

"Give me half-an-hour," said James.

"You got it. But you're not out of here by then, you room don't get cleaned today. You hear me?"

"I hear you," said James as he went through into the bathroom. After all, this was New York. What did he expect for two hundred and fifty bucks a day?

Horatio greeted him like an old friend, buzzing him in almost before he'd rung the bell.

"I know," said James. "Sign the book."

"Right. Then you can go straight on up."

"Is Ms. Francis around?"

"She's out to lunch," said Horatio. "See, here's her name where she signed out."

"Very efficient," said James.

Upstairs, he met Ted, a neat man in his sixties wearing a thousand-dollar suit. He handed James the key and a sheet of paper. It was a typed list. James looked at it. There were four main headings.

Grand Central Station.

Port Authority Bus terminal.

JFK Airport.

La Guardia Airport.

Under each heading was a short description of exactly where a bank of lockers could be located in each facility.

"I don't get it," said James.

"These lockers are designed for people who want to leave stuff a few hours, overnight, or even a week maybe. Not real valuable stuff, for that they use a safe deposit. We're taking about a suitcase or an overnight bag. For example, a guy rents locker number 39 at Grand Central, what chance is there he's going to make a mistake and try to use the key on locker number 39 at JFK?"

"No chance," said James.

"That's what the locker-maker figured. So he cut a few corners and saved a few bucks by duplicating some of the locks, which is no big deal, as long as they're not at the same location."

"No big deal for me, either," said James. "I'll try them all."

"It might be worth bearing in mind that opening a locker that has already been rented to somebody is a criminal offense."

"I'll bear it in mind."

"There's another snag," said Ted.

"There usually is."

"You've got the manufacturer's list for New York. That's it."

"That's all I want."

"What you're looking for couldn't be in New Jersey or Connecticut? Or Oshkosh Wisconsin, for that matter?"

"It could."

"In that case, you're up shit creek. Because that key could match locker 39 at facilities with lockers in other cities provided by the same manufacturer."

"Right," said James. He glanced at the list again, before stuffing it in his pocket along with the key.

"I suppose there's not much point in me asking what you're hoping to find," asked Ted.

"I'm grateful for what you've done," said James. "But you're right. There's not much point in asking."

❖   ❖   ❖

On his way downstairs, he detoured to Wanda's office. She still hadn't returned from lunch. The lingering smell of her perfume was all that was needed to run him on again. He thought about leaving her a note, then decided against it. He'd call her later.

"She just called in," said Horatio as James went to sign out.

"Who?"

"Ms. Francis. She just called in."

"And?"

"She said she wasn't coming back from lunch until later. She asked if you were still here and I told her you were upstairs and was there any message and she hung up on me. Didn't say goodbye or nothing, the stuck-up bitch."

James signed out, told Horatio to have a nice day and walked out into the midday heat. He couldn't find a cab, so he hopped a bus heading downtown on fifth. He got out at 45th Street and walked over to Grand Central Station.

Ted's list directed him to a large bank of lockers on the South side of the main concourse. It was a wasted trip. Locker number 39 was not being used. He tried his key anyway, just to make sure he wasn't on some kind of fool's errand. It worked. Okay. One down, three to go. He walked cross town on 42nd Street to the Bus Terminal. The directions were a little confusing, but eventually he found the bank of lockers he was looking for. Number 39 was in use. Feeling like a downmarket safecracker, he opened the locker with his key. Inside was a canvas bag. He could hardly go through it standing here, so he took it from the locker and carried it to another part of the terminal, where he unzipped it. A man's shaving stuff, a pair of dirty pajamas and two pornographic magazines. He stuffed everything back in the bag and replaced it in the locker. Two down, two to go. He hailed a cab outside the bus station and told the driver he wanted to go to LaGuardia. Then the cab should wait to maybe take him on to Kennedy.

"What's a matter? You don' know which airport your fuckin' airplane's at?" said the cabby, a middle-aged black guy with a squashed face and ferocious body odor.

"I'm not flying," said James.

"So, why are you going to two fuckin' airports?"

"You want to take me or not?"

"You got the money?"

"I've got it," said James, starting to lose his patience.

"So, stop fuckin' around and get in the cab."

The cabby wanted to know which route James wanted to take to the airport.

"Just don't take me through any tunnel of New York's tunnels." The combination of the heat, humidity and the cabby's body odor in one of New York's tunnels, didn't bear contemplating.

"What's a matter? You got one of them phobias against tunnels?"

"I like bridges," said James.

"So, which one? Tribourough or Queens?"

"I don't care."

"You should care, mister. Triborough's quicker but they got a toll. Queensboro don't cost fuck all except maybe on the clock."

"Go the quicker route," said James.

"You got it."

They went the Tribourough route and got caught in a two mile back up just across the bridge. The cabby took the opportunity to tell James that he hated his job, his home life was shit, his wife was cheating on him and his eldest boy only stayed in high school 'cause that's where his main market was for the crack he was pushing.

"You got kids?" asked the cabby.

"No, I don't."

"Take my advice. Keep it that way. You knock up your old lady, have her get rid of it. If she don't, strangle the little bastard soon as he sticks his head out. Kids is the fuckin' worst, man."

"I'll remember," said James.

"On the other hand, there's all kinds 'a problems."

"There sure are," said James. No point in being unfriendly.

"I mean like, you got one. Right?"

"Not me," said James.

"So how come some asshole's following you?"

At first James didn't believe him. The cabby told him that the black Cadillac limo half-a-dozen cars back had been on their tail at least since 96th Street and Second Avenue, and maybe ever since they left the bus station, but it was at 96th, and Second that he first noticed it because he near as fuckall shot a red and he looked in the mirror to make sure there weren't no cop hanging around and he saw the Cadillac pull out from behind a couple of cars that was stoppin' for the red and damn near ran down half-a-dozen pedestrians, which he'd only have done if he'd wanted to stay close to the cab and he'd been watching them on and off ever since, and if they wasn't following this cab, then his name wasn't Mustapha Zee, which it had been ever since he joined the Muslims back in seventy five.

James still wasn't convinced, so Mustapha Zee took the first off ramp they came to. The Cadillac followed. He pulled up outside a convenience store. The caby got out of the cab, went into the store and came out a couple of minutes later munching on a candy bar. Meantime, James had been watching the Cadillac. It had pulled up half a block past the store and was now parted curbside, its darkened windows giving nothing away. Mustapha Zee climbed back into the driver's seat.

"Wanna piece of candy bar?" he said.

"No, thanks."

"You believe me now?" asked Mustapha.

"Ninety percent," said James. "Let's go."

Mustapha started the cab once more and pulled out. He passed the Cadillac which started up immediately, slotting in behind them once more. James had a vague glimpse of the driver and a front seat passenger, neither of whom he recognized. Maybe there were people in the back, he couldn't tell.

"Now you fucking convinced?"

"One hundred percent," said James.

"So, you want I should lose them?"

"Could you do that?"

"No problem. I'll just drive on back to 125th Street and Second Avenue, that's Harlem, man, and I'll park in back of an empty lot I know 'bout. It'll take three minutes for their wheels to disappear. Meantime, some other dudes of my acquaintance will be winching out their engine and if they get out to complain, the brother will stomp on them."

It sounded tempting. But, right now, it was more important to know who they were and what they wanted. Also, he had an idea how they might have gotten onto him, and he didn't like it one little bit.

"Let's go to the airport," he said.

Mustapha Zee was beginning to enjoy himself. "What are you into, Mister?"

"CIA," said James.

"Holy shit! Who are the dudes in the Caddy?"

"Foreign agents."

"What country?"

James wasn't sure where Mustapha's loyalties might lie, so he played it safe. "South Africa," he said.

Mustapha dropped James outside the main arrival building. He told James he would wait for as long as it took. And if there was anything else, he could do t help, just name it. James told him what might be required. Could Mustapha handle it?

"If I can help stick it to those South African motherfuckers, you've got it pal."

James scribbled his name and address on a scrap of paper and handed it, with the locker key and $100 bill, to Mustapha. Then he got out of the cab and pretended to pay what was on the clock. Mustapha drove off. James let him get just out of sight before he turned and started towards the terminal.

As James walked into the building, he was aware of two guys getting out of the Cadillac, which had parked thirty feet behind the cab, one from the back, one from the front, the driver stayed behind the wheel. A three-man team. James was impressed.

The blast of the air conditioning in the terminal building reminded James how stifling it was outside. The adrenalin was pumping so hard, he'd forgotten to perspire. The two guys followed James, keeping a safe distance, as he walked to a bank of phones, just beating an old lady to the only free one. There he dug for change and called S.S.S. The two men took up a position at the far end of the line of phones. They also got lucky, elbowing out the same old lady, who gave up and wandered off. One of them pretended to make a call. They were young and beefy, not unlike Gary and Bill. Perhaps Jackson Webber ran a stable of hefty young fags just to do this dirty work for him.

When the Schiner office answered the phone, James asked to speak with Horatio. "Did Wanda Francis get back from lunch yet?"

"Who wants to know?"

James identified himself.

"Oh. Hi there Mr. Reed. No, sir, she ain't back yet and the shit's hitting the fan upstairs." Horatio sounded pleased that Wanda might be in some kind of trouble.

"She usually this late?"

"Nope. You wanna know something. I think she's in some kind of bind. Like remember I told you she called while you was still here?"

"I remember," said James.

"Okay. So she sounded real uptight. Not like madam cool she makes out to be most of the time."

James thanked him and hung up. He called Wanda's home number. There was no answer. He called the Gramercy Park Hotel and asked if there were any messages for him. There were two, both from a Miss Francis. She had called at twelve thirty. Would he please call back, it was urgent. She called again at one. She was about to go to lunch but it was very important she speak to him, she understood he had a one thirty meeting at the office, would he please wait there until she returned. James broke the connection but kept the dead phone to his ear while he thought about the ramifications. It took him fifteen seconds to come up with a scenario.

Gary had found out from Landers that James would be contacting the Schiner office in New York. He, or Bill, or one of their cohorts had called Wanda and asked if she knew the whereabouts of one James Reed. She could have said no, but being Wanda, she probably said that she did, but the caller could whistle up a tree before she told him. So, they waited outside the office until she went to lunch and they grabbed her.

Where's James Reed lady? Tell us or we'll get very unpleasant. Maybe they banged her around just a little to prove they meant what they said. What could she do but tell them he's due at the office at 1:30 for a meeting?

What kind of meeting?

Something to do with a key.

What kind of key, lady?

The key to a public locker.

That means Reed sold us the wrong key.

So, they were waiting outside when he came out of Schiner's. They followed him to Grand Central, where they saw him open an empty, unrented locker. Next, they followed him to the bus terminal, where he opened a locker and went through the contents of an overnight bag. The guy's crazy.

Now they've followed him to La Guardia. Hopefully he'll open another locker. And this time they might get lucky. As soon as he grabs anything out of a locker, they'll be all over him.

But right now, that wasn't James's main problem. What had happened to Wanda had priority. That was something he was going to deal with right away.

The two guys were still at their station, one of them murmuring into an empty phone, both of them doing their best not to look in James's direction. He replaced the phone and started towards them. Their lack of interest in him was total, both of them looking everywhere but in his direction. They might have been heavy in the muscle department but they weren't too bright in any of the other. Or so James sincerely hoped.

"Hi fellas!" he said, stopping next to them. Close up they looked even more like Gary and Bill than he'd first thought. Around twenty-four or five, both a shade over six feet tall, they looked like a couple of college football players. If they heard James's greeting, they gave no sign. One of them continued to hold the phone to his ear, the other stared off into the middle distance.

"You wanna tell me what's happened to the lady, then providing I'm satisfied, we can all go home."

"I'm sorry. Are you talking to me, sir?

Sir! James liked that. Polite. "I'm talking to the both of you."

The guy on the phone now condescended to look at James. "Sir?"

"You heard me fellas. Where is the lady?"

The two guys looked at each other, then back to James.

"I'm sorry, sir. I don't know what you're talking about."

"Then I'd better explain. I'd like you to call your boss and tell him that I've already picked up what he's looking for. If you two assholes had been doing your job properly, you'd have spotted that at the bus terminal. Not only did I pick it up, but I also got rid of it. When you've told him all that, tell him that unless I can be convinced that the lady is safe, and in one piece, then he should make sure he gets his copy of the *New York Times* tomorrow because he'll likely be all over the front page."

The two guys flashed at look at each other. Then back to James.

"I'm sorry, sir. We still don't know what you're talking about."

"Suit yourselves," said James. He turned and started away.

"Wait a moment, sir."

"Go fuck yourselves," said James.

"Sir!"

James turned back to face them. The one who had been seated at the phone now stood up alongside his companion. The sheer bulk of the two of them side-by-side, made them look four times as intimidating, especially as they decided to hell with being polite any longer.

"You're full of shit," said the guy who'd been on the phone. He was a shade smaller than his companion. He had a cast in one eye which made him look slightly crazy. "We watched you at the bus terminal. You got zilch."

"So be it," said James. He started away again.

"We'll call him," said the other one, quickly.

"The fuck we will!" said the companion.

James looked from one to the other. "Why don't you go talk to your buddy, the driver, and take a vote on it. He's entitled. He fucked up most of all."

The guy with the eye problem still wasn't convinced. "You didn't pick up anything at the bus station."

"Then you've got nothing to worry about," said James. "Except Jackson Webber."

"Who the fuck is Jackson Webber?"

James pretended to lose his patience. "Okay, guys. That's it!"

"Hold it! Hold it! Okay. Say you did pick up something at the bus station. How'd you get rid of it? We've been eyeballing you all the way."

"Guess," said James.

They had to give it some thought, but eventually one of them came up with the answer. "The cabby."

"Right on," said James.

"Let's go make the call," said the other one.

The one with the crazy eye made the call. The other stayed with James, far enough away from the telephone so the conversation could not be overheard. Finally, he hung up and beckoned James and his companion over.

"He says to wait."

"Wait for what?"

"For him to call back. Two minutes, he said."

James tried to work it out. Whoever crazy eye had called, it wasn't Webber. Now Webber was being contacted. So they waited. A young guy who tried to use the phone was told to fuck off. Three minutes later, it rang. Crazy eye identified himself, listened for a moment, then hung up.

"He says to turn her loose."

"Okay. So, do it," said the companion.

He dialed another number. He cupped the receiver and spoke quietly so James couldn't overhear. Finally, he hung up.

"Let's go," he said.

James walked with them out of the terminal building. As they headed towards the Cadillac, the rear door opened and Wanda Francis stumbled out. She stood for a moment, looking around as though she had no idea where she was. The two guys ignored her completely. They climbed into the car, which drove off a moment later.

Meanwhile Wanda had spotted James.

"You son of a bitch," she said.

She looked in one piece. "Are you okay?" he asked, taking her arm.

"Oh sure! I mean this kind of thing happens every day. I want a drink," she said.

"So, lets get one." He watched for a moment as the cab driven by Mustapha Zee swept past him, after the Cadillac.

"What are you waiting for, for Christ's sake. I want it now," said Wanda.

"You've got it," he said, steering he toward the terminal building.

They were sitting at a bar in the terminal, where fliers were drinking some courage before getting on a plane.

"They were waiting for me when I went out to lunch. I would have waited for you but I have to pee Prune at lunchtime. God! He'll have messed in the apartment." She thought about it for a moment before deciding there wasn't anything she could do about it. "They bundled me into the back of their car and said if I didn't tell them where they could find you, they'd take me to an empty lot and gang bang me. And after they'd all stuck their dicks in me, they'd start sticking in other things, like tire irons and monkey wrenches."

"So, you told them."

"Bet your ass."

"You told them I would be at the office at one thirty?"

"Yep!"

"And that I was asking about a locker key."

"I did. Listen, I'd have told them anything they wanted. If I didn't know the answer, I'd have made it up. Okay?"

"Okay," said James.

"Then I said, please can I go now? But they wanted me to stay with them so I could identify you when you showed up."

"Which you did."

"Which I did. I asked if I could go, but they said they wanted to hang onto me until they'd done whatever business they had with you. Then they were going to gang bang me anyway. I was scared."

"I don't blame you. Have another drink."

"I don't want another drink. I want to go home and I want you out of my life."

She called the office from the airport bar and spoke to Abe Schiner. She apologized for not showing up after lunch but she'd felt poorly and please, as it was now close to four thirty, would he mind very much if she didn't show at all today? While she was on the phone, James bought her another drink, which she said she didn't want but she drank anyway. Then he took her home in a cab.

"Maybe I'd better come upstairs with you," he said, she paid off the cab.

"Why?"

"Make sure there's nobody waiting."

She agreed he could come upstairs as far as the front door. He watched her unlock the door and say hello to a hysterical Prune, who immediately dumped a load in the hallway.

"Poor baby. Did Mommy forget to come home to take him out for his lunchtime walkies?"

James followed her in, now he offered to take Prune out while she cleaned up the mess.

"Take my key, I'm going to have a shower. I feel dirty all over."

James took the front door key from her. "Better tell the guy on the desk to let me in and out."

She called down to the desk and told the guy on duty that James Reed was a friend and could come and go. She hung up and turned back to James. "But don't let that give you ideas. As soon as you get back, you leave. Understand?"

He did.

Downstairs, the guy behind the desk had decided to be friendly.

"Hi there, Mr. Reed," he said as James came out of the elevator.

"I put your name in the book here."

"What book is that?" James wanted to know.

"Names of people what can come and go without having to get permission all the time, like Ms. Francis wanted."

It wasn't at all like what Ms. Francis wanted, but James wasn't about to let on, especially as he intended to change her mind about him staying. He and Prune took a turn round the block. There was a flower shop on 67th where he spent close to $100. Next door was a liquor store, where he asked for a bottle of Dom Perignon.

The middle-aged guy behind the counter recognized Prune.

"If you're buying for Ms. Francis, she prefers Perrier-Jouet."

James bought the Perrier-Jouet and asked for it to be gift wrapped. The guy eyed the flowers while he was doing it. "My, what a lucky lady she is," he said. "Mark you, she deserves it. She's a lovely person. Don't you think?"

James agreed that he thought she was a lovely person.

"Something nice should come into her life," said the guy as he finished wrapping the champagne. He looked a James critically as he handed him the package.

"Yes. Well let's all hope she doesn't have to wait too long."

Prune hadn't had any lunch and was in a hurry now to get home. James was in a hurry too, but for a different reason.

"Hi there, Mr. Reed," said the guy on the door, eyeing what James was carrying. "Looks like party time."

James let himself into the apartment, bolted the door behind him and walked through into the bedroom. Steam was still curling around the half open bathroom door and he could hear the shower running. He pushed open the door to the bathroom. He could see Wanda's naked body out of focus behind the shower glass, pink with a smudge of dark.

"I'm back," he called, above the sound of the water.

"Goodbye," she said loudly.

"I've got something for you."

"I can't hear you."

"I've bought you a present," he bellowed.

The shower turned off. The door opened and she stuck her head around. "What did you say?" Then she saw the orchids and the gift box. "What's that?"

"For you," he said.

"Bastard," she said.

He shrugged modestly. "Best I could do at short notice."

"I suppose you'll be telling me you want to take a shower next."

"I want to take a shower."

She thought about it for a moment. For one brief second, James thought he might have blown it. "So, what are you waiting for," she said finally.

Sex in a shower, like sex anyplace else, can be good, bad or indifferent. This was good. Their bodies, wet and slippery with hot water, soap and perspiration, slid over, around and into each other like separate parts of a well-oiled, perfectly tuned machine. And when that was finished, James risked a hernia by carrying her into the bedroom where, soaking wet, he dropped her on the bed. He broke open the gift wrapping, popped the cork on the champagne and poured some into her navel. It overflowed and ran down into the dark thatch of her pubic har.

"Cheers," he said. He started to lick it up.

"Lower," she said.

He did as he was asked. Fifteen minutes and an aching jaw later, she pushed him away.

"You and I have got to have a talk," she said.

"What about?"

She reversed her position. "I'll tell you later. Mummy told me it was rude to talk with your mouth full."

"Bully for Mummy," said James.

Afterwards, she fetched an ice bucket and a couple of glasses from the kitchen and still naked, smelling of sex, she climbed back into bed beside James. She poured two glasses and handed one to James. "A toast," she said.

"To us?"

"There's no such thing as us," she said.

"So, what do we drink to?"

She thought about it. "How about what might have been."

"Why can't what might have been become what might actually be?"

"No chance. I have a well-ordered life, me and Prune. I like it. I like the security and the comfort of knowing where I am and what I'm doing every day. I go to the office, I come home, I've got my place in the country that I visit on weekends. I've got a couple of longtime girlfriends, who I like a lot. We go to exercise classes and movies and sometimes to singles bars, strictly for laughs. I meet nice ordinary men from time-to-time and occasionally I get laid. Not as often as I'd like perhaps, but that's okay. Maybe you think all that's boring."

"Why should I think that is boring?"

"Because your own life is such a goddamn mess?"

"Who said it was a mess?"

"Come on! I mean, who were those creeps? What did they want?"

"They wanted me."

"I know that. Why did they want you?"

"You really want to know?"

She thought about it for a moment. Then she shook her head. "No, I don't want to know."

It was just as well because he wouldn't have told her. But now that he'd been reminded of the day's happenings, maybe he should do something about it. "You mind if I make a phone call?" he asked.

"Providing it's not to a girlfriend. You want I should leave the room?"

"Stay where you are. I've got plans for later." He dialed the number Mustapha Zee had given him, a woman answered, and asked to speak to Mustapha.

"He ain't home yet. Who's callin'?"

"Is this Mrs. Zee?"

"This is Mrs. Thomason. Just 'cause my husband calls him-self crazy names, it don't mean I got to."

"What time does he normally get home, Mrs. Thomason?"

"You ain't the police, are you?"

"Nope."

"Okay, then. If he ain't doin' the night shift, he should be home any time now. You want he should call you?"

"I'll call him, thanks." He hung up and held his glass towards Wanda who poured him another champagne.

"What happens now?"

"Now we have another shower and we get dressed and we go out and get something to eat."

"I've got a better idea."

She climbed out of bed and still naked, she disappeared in the direction of the kitchen. A couple of minutes later, James heard pots and pans being rattled. She was going to cook dinner for him. He was home and dry.

He showered again, wrapped a towel around his middle and wandered into the kitchen. She'd tied an apron on over her nakedness. James thought it was one of the most erotic things he'd seen all year. He made a grab for her but she evaded him. "Eat first," she said.

As he moved away, the towel slipped from around his middle. She watched him as he picked it up and retied it. Then she shook her head slowly. "I've got to be crazy," she said.

He went back into the living room, chased Prune off a chair, sat down and called Mustapha again. This time, the cabby answered the phone himself.

"You sure them dudes was South African? They looked and talked just like your regular American honky rednecks."

"They work for the South Africans was what I said."

"That figures. Just so long as I know what I'm into. So, I followed 'em back to this place on 35th Street. I parked outside and I waited while they all went in. I'm still waiting half an hour later so I think, what the fuck, I'll go have a look inside. It's a kind of gym, high-tech exercise equipment, punchin' bags and wall-to-wall fags with no necks and muscles like Schwarzenegger. Some guy comes up to me and asks what I want and I tell him I'm considerin' getting' in shape and I'm just checkin' the place out 'cause by the look of things a place like this could be dangerous to guys' health less he knows what he's doin'. He tells me they don't take no blacks. So, I said I'd report him to the race relations and he said I could do whatever I fucking liked, they still don't take blacks and if I didn't want to get my head busted with one of his crutches, I should beat it. So, I beat it."

"Crutches?"

"Those metal things you stick under your arm when you got a broken leg."

"I know what crutches are."

"I still got your key. What do you want me to do with it?"

"You can drive me out to JFK tomorrow morning."

"Where do I pick you up?"

James wondered whether Wanda would want to kick him out at six thirty a.m. again. He decided to take a chance. He gave Mustapha the address of the apartment building.

"Outside at eight thirty a.m.," he said.

"You got it," said Mustapha.

The good smells coming out of the kitchen proved to be misleading. Apart from a red wine, which was excellent, dinner was heavy on the starch and light on the flavor. He slipped a couple of mouthfuls to the dog, under the table. Wanda watched him play around with what was growing cold on his plate.

"I know," she said. "I'm an awful cook."

"It's okay," he said.

"No, it's not."

"You're right. It's not." He pushed his plate aside.

"You're not much of a catch yourself," she said, immediately going on the defensive.

"Wait 'til you know me better."

"I don't think I want to. It's too dangerous."

"Today's events were a one-off," said James.

"I don't believe you. You've got that look about you. Kind of lost, lone wolf type look. Guys with that look are always into some kind of trouble." She stood up and started collecting the plates. "If you're still hungry, you'll have to call out for something."

"I'm not hungry," he lied. He could always get himself a sandwich later. He helped her with the dishes and scraped clean a pan she'd burned. Afterwards, she said she was going to wash her hair, would he do her a favor and take Prune for his last walk. It would save her having to get dressed again. She disappeared into the bathroom. He collected the front door key and, because he wasn't going to be more than five minutes, he didn't bother to double-lock the door behind him. There was a new guy on duty downstairs, somebody James hadn't seen before. He was a black guy with a pock marked face and a ready smile. "Hey Prune dog, how you goin'?

Prune obviously approved. He wagged his tail. The black guy looked at James, speculatively. "No need to ask how you're doin'."

"I'll be doing better if I can get something to eat," said James.

The guy directed him to a hamburger joint three and half blocks away, where he ordered a king-sized to go and ate as he walked Prune a couple of times around the block. He even scooped her poop into a plastic bag, feeling very domesticated about the whole set up. He started to speculate how Wanda might enjoy a life on the beach. He walked back along Broadway and tuned down 66th Street. Prune was in a hurry to get home now, dragging on the lead. James was felling so pleased with himself that he even called a 'good night' to the cop in the shelter outside the Chinese embassy. The cop looked at him as if he was crazy.

He didn't even notice the car parked right outside the entrance to the apartment building, not until the window at the front went down.

"Hey, mister?" the guy inside asked. James turned toward the car. "You got the time?"

"Sure." He angled his watch to catch the light spilling from the apartment entrance. As he did so he recognized the man as one of the guys from the airport. He started to turn.

"In the back, buddy." The voice came from behind him. At the same time, he felt the jab of something hard just about his kidney.

The driver, who had asked him the time, reached back and opened the rear door of the car. Okay, James Reed, tough guy, there's a cop twenty-five yards up the street, there's a doorman in the building behind you, and there's a group of kids coming out of the Juilliard School on the opposite side of the street. Are you going to let yourself be hijacked with all that going on around you?

"Don't even think about it," said the man standing behind him.

James did as he was told. He released his hold on Prune's lead. The dog scampered into the building. James bent low and got into the car. The guy with the gun, James assumed it was a gun, got in behind him. Almost before he'd closed the door, the car was on the move.

SIX

They took him to the gymnasium on 35th Street. It was atop a two-story parking building. It consisted of one large plastic dome, connected to two smaller ones at each end. Stairs led up the side through an airlock door with the sign MIDTOWN FITNESS, STRICTLY MEMBERS ONLY. Like Mustapha had said, the place was full of high-tech exercise equipment. The lights were on, but the fitness freaks had all gone home. The only person there was Gary. As James was bundled into the place, he came out of a small office, supported on metal crutches. He had plaster on his leg from ankle-to-knee, and on his arm from wrist-to-elbow. He was a mess and looked mad enough to spit nails. James figured there was no point in starting on the 'what's the meaning of this outrage' scenario, so he kept quiet.

"Have you searched him?" Gary asked.

"He was walking the dog for Christ's sake, what he gonna be carrying?" said the guy with the crazy eye.

"Do it," said Gary.

"If you're looking for the key, forget it," said James.

Gary told the guy to go ahead. He patted James down efficiently and came up with nothing other than Wanda's apartment keys and James's wallet. Nobody seemed interested in either and the guy handed them back to James.

"I told you there was no key," said James.

"Strap his hands," said Gary.

A leather strap was produced and James's wrist were strapped securely behind his back.

"Sit him over there," said Gary, nodding towards a leather covered bench. They walked James to the bench and pushed him down. "Strap his legs."

They strapped his legs to the legs of the bench, Gary limped over and checked on what they'd done. Apparently, he was satisfied.

"You guys can beat it," he said.

"We'll stick around," said crazy eye.

"No, you won't," said Gary. "I'll see you tomorrow."

The guys didn't argue. They just left. The airlock door hissed shut behind them, leaving only the silence of a New York night, which by any other standards, was pretty noisy.

"Your employer is going to be real pissed off at you," said James.

"Is that right?"

"Like I told your guys out at the airport, I'm ready to spread that stuff all over the newspapers."

Gary looked at him a long moment. "I don't believe you. Neither do I give a fuck. This is you and me. Personal."

Bad news, decided James. If Gary truly didn't care, he was in deep shit. Not least of his concerns was the fact that Gary's guys had made no attempt to hide where they were bringing him. To James, that meant Gary figured it didn't matter one way or the other because, by the end of the evening, James Reed was going to in no position to do anything about anything.

"What's personal between you and me?" asked James, playing for time.

"How about a busted arm and a busted leg?"

"I'd have thought that was an occupational hazard for a guy in your line of work."

"Dead isn't an occupation hazard," said Gary. He scratched his arm just above the plaster with his good hand. "Fucking itching is driving me crazy," he said to nobody in particular. As he readjusted one of his crutches, he was off balance for a brief second.

He still wasn't too secure with them. James was going to need an edge pretty soon and right now, that's the only one he could see.

"Who's dead?" James asked. Time was what he needed now.

"Don't give me that crap."

"Megan McCoy is dead Paul Menzies is dead. Who else that I don't know about."

"How about Bill Goodge?"

"I don't know a Bill Goodge."

"You cut off his ear and stove in his face."

"I didn't know he was dead."

Gary managed to support himself on one crutch only. He swung the other at James, catching him across the bridge of his nose. Luckily it was made of aluminum or it might have caved in James's skull. As it was, all his light went out for a moment or two. He would have toppled off the bench, but the straps around his legs kept him in a more or less upright position. When he could focus again, Gary had stuck the crutch back under this arm and had moved closer, looking down at him.

"Me and Bill were good buddies. We went way back. You understand what I'm saying? We were close, man, really close. So, when I hear that you offed him, I want to do something about it. Difference between you and Bill, is I'm not going to stop with your ear. I'm gonna make a cut here, a slice there, nice and slow. And when I've finished, I'm going to put a bullet in your skull and I'm gonna dump you in the East River instead of setting you alight."

"That wasn't Bill Goodge," said James. His nose was bleeding and his lip was beginning to swell.

"What wasn't?"

"The guy who burned to death in California. It was Paul Menzies."

"Says who?"

"Says the LAPD, says the coroner, says me who identified the body. And probably says your friend Bill when he shows because he's the guy I figure did it."

"Why would you figure that?" At least he'd got Gary's interest.

"He told me when I saw him. He said the kid would be taken care of. Guaranteed."

"So how come I'm not in on this?"

"You were flat on your back in traction is why," James hawked up some blood and spat it out on the floor.

Gary was still doubtful. "He was supposed to pick me up from the hospital. He never showed."

"Maybe he just changed his mind. Maybe he got nervous and split. Maybe you two had a lover's spat. What do I know!"

"He wouldn't do that," said Gary. He thought about it some more before deciding the wasn't going to buy it. "You're full of shit."

"You don't believe me, call L.A."

Gary looked at his watch, a maneuver which nearly made him fall over. "Who am I gonna call? It's around eight p.m. in LA."

"Lieutenant Micklehaus of the LAPD. Or, if you don't like talking to cops, call the downtown morgue and ask to speak to Alvin Weeks. Then put me on the line.

For a moment, James didn't think Gary was going to buy it. Then he hobbled off to fetch a telephone with a long cord from the office. He put the phone on the bench next to James. "What's the number?"

"Call information. Area code 213."

Gary dialed the number and asked for the number of the L.A. County morgue in downtown Los Angeles. He thanked the operator politely, broke the connection and started to dial again.

"You're going to have to untie me," said James. Gary didn't even bother responding to this remark. He finished dialing, checked to see if the number was ringing, then he put the phone to James ear. By hunching his shoulders and twisting his neck, James was able to hold it in place. Gary hobbled off to the glassed-in office area. By the time he picked up the extension, the phone had been answered at the other end.

"County morgue."

"Let me speak to Alvin Weeks," said James. Blood was leaking from his nose all over the phone.

"Alvin ain't on nights. Who is this?"

"LAPD, Lieutenant Micklehaus," said James. He saw Gary look at him from the front office. "I want some info on an ID a few days back."

"How many days?"

"Three," said James.

"What do you want to know?"

"ID made by one James Reed of a male, Caucasian, accidental death by burning."

"What about it?"

"Who was the stiff?"

"Hang on."

The guy was away for what seemed like a long time. James' neck had started to ache from the way it was twisted. He needed to clear his throat and spit out some more blood. If the call didn't finish soon, he was going to drop the phone. Finally, the guy came back on the line. "You still there?"

"I'm here," said James.

"Corpse identified by James Reed as that of Paul Menzies."

"Cause of death?"

"Like you said. Burning. I got the photos here. Man, he was done to a crisp."

James thanked him and allowed the phone to slip out from under his ear. He hawked and spat blood again. Not so much this time, but his mouth was beginning to feel like a piece of raw liver. He was still trying to straighten the crick in his neck as Gary came hobbling back from the office. He picked up the phone from where James had dropped it and replaced it on its cradle.

"Satisfied?" said James.

"So, where is Bill Goodge?"

James decided the time had come for him to show a little aggression. "How the hell should I know? Ask your boss. He's the guy who gave the orders. Maybe he got nervous and he got some other guys who work for him to take care of your buddy Bill the same way he took care of Menzies just in case Bill started shooting off his mouth. What the hell do I know about big wheel operators like Webber?" He was building up a good head of steam, even if it was acting. "By now, he could have got more guys to take care of the guys who took care of Bill. Then he'll get more guys to take care of them. It could go on forever. And somewhere down the line, he'll remember you and you'll get yours, too. What do you want from me, for Christ's sake? I don't know shit." He was practically shouting by now, spraying blood over a fairly wide area. He pretended to take a grip on himself, calm down. "But if you let me out of here, I might be able to find something out."

"No way," said Gary. But James could see that he'd gotten through to him.

"Knocking me off is not going to achieve anything."

"Neither is letting you go."

Okay, thought James. Keep at it. At least he's into discussion. "Look at it this way. You can't do anything for yourself, and those guys you've got working for you, they can't see further than their muscles. I'm your best shot."

"You're right about one thing. I can't take a piss without falling over. Why'd you go and break my leg?"

James knew he was safe now. "It seemed like a good idea at the time. You were trying to kick the shit out of me."

"We should have offed you up front. Saved everyone a heap of aggravation."

"Especially Webber."

"Fuck him," said Gary. He had moved round behind James. Now he started to unbuckle the strap around his wrists. The strap fell free, "You can do your own legs." He started towards the office as James unbound his legs.

"Where's the washroom?" he called to Gary.

"Out back. You wanna drink?"

"In a minute."

James walked through to the lock room that smelled of sweat and liniment. He looked at his reflection in the mirror over the basins. He looked worse than he had when Bill had socked him with a piece of iron pipe. His face was covered with blood and his upper lip had swollen to almost twice its size. Much more of this and the was going to look like Quasimodo. He rinsed the blood off his face. He couldn't do anything about the stains on his shirt or jacket and he couldn't do anything about his lip. Maybe it would go down in time. He sure hoped so. But, right now, that was the least of his worries. Number one was getting clear of Gary as soon as possible. Once Gary started talking, it had taken James exactly thirty seconds to figure out what had happened to Bill Goodge. He didn't want Gary figuring out the same thing, at least not until he had put some distance between the two of them.

He joined Gary in the office. Gary was seated behind the desk, his crutches standing against the wall behind him. As James came in, he pointed at a bourbon bottle and told him to help himself.

"Sit down," he said to James. James sat in a straight back chair against the partition wall. "So, convince me I should turn you loose."

"I thought you already had," said James.

"Wrong," said Gary. His hand appeared from below the top of the desk, he was holding a gun, a .38 revolver. "All I did was untie you."

"Come on," said James. "Don't start in on me again. Your buddy's not dead. That means I didn't kill him. What do you want with me?"

"You said you'd find out where he's at."

"I said I'd try."

"How are you going to go about it?"

"Webber. I'm going to lean on him. Anything you can tell me about him that I don't know will be a help."

"You're the one whose got the dirt on him."

James had forgotten he was supposed to have uncovered the blackmail material, "I hope it makes more sense to him than it does to me," he said. "Any idea how to put this together?"

"Search me. This chick … the one in California … the one me and Bill *didn't* knock off, put together some kind of a file while she was working for him. She was his secretary or something. That's all I know. Our job was to get it back, wherever and whatever. We come to see you. Things get heavy, and I'm up to my ass in plaster. Next thing I hear, Bill is dead. I've got to figure you did it 'cause you're the only contact we made out there."

"How did you hear about it?"

"I got this phone call in the hospital. Some chick."

"What chick?"

"I don't know what chick. A chick. I figured she was from the morgue or the cops or something. Anyway, I check myself out of the hospital and make it over to your place. I'm ready to blow you away there and then. But this old guy says you're in New York and if I want you, I should call this Schiner number. So, I come back here and call and this broad says sure, you're in town, but she's not gonna tell me where you're at. So, I send the two guys to find out. They come on heavy and snatch her. Would you believe that? Anyway, it worked and we find out where you're at and the fact you're chasing around New York with a locker key, the same locker that Webber's just paid five grand for. I call Webber and tell him and he says to stay on you and grab whatever you pull out of the locker. Then I call him again and tell him what you said about the *New York Times* and he says forget the whole thing."

"Why would he do that?"

"Who knows from guys like that. Maybe he figures he'd rather pay up than have the stuff spread all over. Okay, so as far as Webber's concerned, forget it. But as far as I'm concerned, no way. You knocked off Bill."

"Except now you know it wasn't Bill."

"Right. So, where is he?"

"I'll check with Webber."

"What are you going to do? Walk fight up to him and ask where Bill Goodge is at?"

"Something like that," said James. "Don't forget. I've got something he wants very badly. Can I go now?"

Gary looked across the desk at him. The gun was still in his hand, resting on the blotter. After a moment, he shook his head.

"You want to know what I can't figure?"

"Not particularly," said James.

"What's in this for you. Where you fit in. Okay, so you've got some heavy stuff on Webber. But I don't figure you're into blackmail. You're a creep, but not that kind of creep. So, where's the pay day?"

"Job satisfaction," said James.

"Bullshit. You don't even have a job. I know about you. You're a high-class beach bum."

James couldn't argue with him so he said nothing. Apparently, Gary made up his mind. "Okay. You can go." James stood up, but Gary hadn't quite finished. "Soon as you get anything on where Bill's at, you call me here. Okay?"

"Okay."

"So, what are you waiting for. Beat it."

James beat it.

He didn't want to frighten Wanda by turning up looking like a refugee from a slaughterhouse and, since he was only a dozen blocks from Gramercy Park, he headed back to the hotel. The night clerk didn't bat an eyelid when a bloodstained James asked for his key. He handed James his messages, wished him a pleasant night and went back to watching *The Late Late Show*. James checked his messages in the elevator. There was a note from the hotel management reminding him that he had to vacate his room tomorrow. And would he please call Mr. Jackson Webber at his earliest convenience. As soon as he reached his room, he called Webber. The butler answered the phone. No sir, Mr. Webber was sleeping and there was no way that the butler was about to awaken him. Try again tomorrow. It was obvious in the tone of voice that the butler had been sleeping, too, and there was no point in arguing. James hung up and called Wanda. She had to be worried out of her mind. At first, he thought he must be calling the wrong number, then he decided she'd gone out. He was about to give up when she answered, her voice clogged with sleep. James identified himself.

"So?" she wanted to know.

"I wanted to apologize for skipping out," he said.

"Tomorrow." The line went dead.

Okay, so she hadn't been worried. Big deal. He sulked his way into the bathroom where he drew a bath. He threw all his clothes into the corner and climbed into the hot water. By squinching up his knees, he was able to sink low enough in the water so only his nose and eyes were above the surface. The hot water stung his swollen lip, and his wrists were chaffed from where he had been strapped too tightly. He felt like shit, and it wasn't just because of the physical abuse he'd been subjected to. No, what was really pissing him off was the fact that he was here in New York on a fool's errand. He'd climbed on an airplane intent on wreaking some kind of revenge on Jackson Webber and the other persons unknown for murdering poor, dumb, good natured Paul Menzies. Okay, so maybe he'd figured he might extract some financial benefit in the process, but strictly to cover his expenses.

Now all that had gone by the board. A smack in the mouth from a drinks machine looks the same as a smack in the mouth from a steel drawer, especially when the recipient has been burned beyond recognition. Gary had been right, ex-lover Bill Goodge was well and truly dead, and the guy who did it wasn't as dumb and good natured as James had figured.

Paul Menzies was alive and well and had killed Bill.

The first thing he was aware of the next morning was the chambermaid crashing around in the living room next door. He looked at his watch, it was eleven thirty. He'd slept nine straight hours.

"You want to keep it down in there," he called out.

A moment later, she stuck her shiny black face around the door. "You're gonna have to move your ass. It's near twelve noon." Then she saw his face. "Where you been puttin' your mouth, honey?"

"What happens at twelve noon?"

"Pumpkin time for you, honey. You're checkin' out."

"I'm not checking out."

"It says on my list you're checkin' out. Now move it. I got a heap of cleanin' up to do."

James called the front desk and told them he was staying on. They reminded him he had promised to be out by the weekend.

"So sue me," said James.

He chased the maid out, had a quick shower and then called the cab company that employed Mustapha Zee. They tracked him down and told James that he'd be outside the hotel in thirty minutes. Then he called Jackson Webber, only to be told that Mr. Webber had left for the house in Easthampton for the weekend. So, what's the number there, James wanted to know. The butler said he wasn't at liberty do disclose that information but if James would care to leave his name and number, he felt sure

Mr. Webber would return the call as soon as he was able. James left his name. Then he went downstairs to wait for Mustapha.

The cab pulled up five minutes later, by which time James had already worked up a healthy sweat. The temperature was heading for the nineties, same with the humidity. He climbed in the back and wound down the windows. Mustapha smelled almost as angry as he sounded.

"So, where the fuck were you at eight thirty this morning?"

"I'll make it up to you," said James.

"Bet your ass," said Mustapha. Then he saw James's face. "Shit, man, what happened to your face?"

"I got hit with a crutch," said James.

"I told you that place wasn't healthy. Where you wanna go?"

"You got my key?"

Mustapha passed back the lock key.

"Kennedy," said James. "But make sure we are not being tailed."

Mustapha made sure by driving the wrong way up a one-way street for a couple of blocks before swinging onto Second Avenue and taking the Tribourough Bridge route out to the airport.

The locker was empty and unrented. Wherever Megan McCoy had hidden the material that had gotten her killed, it wasn't in New York City. James stuffed the key back in his pocket and rejoined Mustapha, who was parked in an illegal zone outside, arguing with a cop.

"Tell this asshole you're with the CIA, for Christ's sake," he said to James.

"I'm with the CIA," said James, climbing in the back of the cab.

"What did I tell you?" said Mustapha to the cop before driving off.

James looked back and saw the cop writing furiously in his book. "I don't think he believed me," he said.

"Who gives a fuck. What now?"

"I want to locate a guy who works for the city."

"Where you wanna go? City Hall? Civic Center?"

"All I know is his name's McCoy, he's an architect and he works for the city."

"It just so happens I might be of some help in that direction, but not for what's on the clock."

"What have you got in mind?"

"Fifty an hour."

"You've got it," said James, remembering he needed to get his hands on some cash money pretty soon.

Mustapha stopped at a bar halfway back to Manhattan and made a couple of phone calls. It seemed one of the brothers of his acquaintance was hanging out with the chick who worked one of the telephone switchboards at City Hall. If Mustapha wanted to grab himself a beer, the brother would get onto his lady friend and, for a small consideration, try to locate McCoy. Mustapha hardly had time to blow the froth off his beer before he called back. Once he had extracted a promise from Mustapha of a twenty-dollar fee, he gave him a telephone number. Mustapha turned it over to James, who ordered another couple more drinks and made his call. He told the secretary who answered that he wanted to speak to Mr. McCoy, that his name was John James, that it was a personal matter and had to do with McCoy's daughter Patsy.

McCoy came on the line almost immediately, an edge of panic in his voice, "Martin McCoy here. What's she done this time?"

James calmed him down, explaining he was a friend from California, that he'd mislaid her number and he'd dearly like to get in touch.

"She's not in trouble?"

"Not that I know of," said James.

McCoy gave James the number. He was so grateful his daughter wasn't going to be a problem again that when James asked for her address as well, he gave him that too. James dialed Patsy McCoy's number and was answered by a machine telling him to leave his name and number and she'd get back to him. He hung up and because he still had some change, he called Schiner's and asked to speak to Wanda. She was out to lunch. He left his name and said he'd call back then he rejoined Mustapha at the bar.

He called Patsy McCoy's number again, half an hour later. She still wasn't home. He told Mustapha to drive him back to his hotel.

"How much I owe you?" James asked when they arrived.

"Three hours at fifty an hour. That's one hundred and fifty bucks."

"One hour of that we were drinking."

"I don't drink with white folk less they pay me."

James handed him two hundred-dollar bills. "Buy some soap," he said.

Mustapha slipped the bills into his shirt packet. "It's glandular," he said.

"It's dirt," said James. He climbed out of the cab. Mustapha started the engine.

"Hey. Where's my change?" said James starting to lean in the front window.

"This is New York, man. Here cabbies get tips. Have a nice day."

He drove off before James could get in another word.

The hotel had moved his room. Instead of a suite on the fourteenth floor, he now had a small single on the third next to the elevator and overlooking the area where they kept the garbage cans. Jackson Webber had called again, leaving an out-of-town number. James called it. The phone was picked up by a woman who spoke as if she needed surgical work done on her sinuses. James asked to speak to Mr. Webber.

"My husband's playing golf. Can I help?"

"My name is Reed, Mrs. Webber. I'm returning your husband's call."

"He should be home by lunchtime, say half-an-hour."

"Please have him call me, Mrs. Webber. I'll wait right here."

He called Wanda at the office. "Sorry about last night," he said.

"It's not important," she said. When a lady said something wasn't important, it invariably meant it was very important indeed. James hadn't intended mentioning his encounter with Gary, now he changed his mind.

"I bumped into the same guys you did," he said.

It worked. "Oh God! Are you alright?"

"More or less. Did Prune come home okay?"

"The doorman brought him up. He said he just came on into the lobby on his own. Are you sure you're alright?"

"Nothing that won't mend. Can I see you this evening?"

"It's Friday. I'm going to the country."

"When will you be back?"

"Why don't you drive out with me? Lonnie's out of town."

It seemed that Lonnie was the girl with whom she shared ownership of the house in Connecticut. James told her it sounded like a sensational idea and arranged to meet her at the apartment at six p.m. He hung up feeling ridiculously pleased with himself. But back to business. He called Patsy McCoy's number again. Still she didn't answer.

Webber called him twenty minutes later. "Jackson Webber here, Mr. Reed. I just wanted you to know that I had nothing to do with the abduction of the young lady yesterday. Those men, whoever they were, exceeded their authority. However, I'd like you to bear in mind that the responsibility for what happened is on your doorstep."

"What were they supposed to do? Kidnap me instead?"

Webber obviously wasn't into sarcasm, he ignored James's remark completely. "If you remember, I paid you five thousand dollars for a locker key. You cheated me, Mr. Reed."

"You're right, Mr. Webber, I cheated you."

"You have located the locker to which the key belongs, I understand."

"Right."

"And you are acquainted with the information therein." He talked like an attorney lecturing a recalcitrant client.

"I am."

"May I ask what your intentions are?"

"You may."

There was a long silence. Finally. "Well …?"

"Well what?"

"What use do you intend making of the material?"

"I haven't made up my mind yet."

"You're quite despicable, Mr. Reed. I suppose you realize that."

"At least I don't go around having people killed."

"What's that supposed to imply?"

"Paul Menzies."

"What about him?"

"Didn't you instruct one of your gay thugs to take care of him?"

Webber sounded genuinely shocked. "Paul's dead?"

"I didn't say that. I said you ordered him taken care of."

"But I … is he dead?"

"Does it matter?"

A long pause. "I suppose not," Webber said.

"It must be great to have a clear conscience," said James. He hung up. Webber was back to him inside a minute.

"I think we should have a talk, you and I," he said.

"I'm listening," said James.

"Not on the phone. Would it be convenient for you to come out to Easthampton this afternoon?"

There wasn't much point in being bloody-minded, and as long as Patsy McCoy wasn't answering her phone, he had nothing else to do.

"How do I get there?"

"I'll arrange transport. Would you prefer car or helicopter?"

James hated helicopters. "Car would be fine." Then he had a better idea. "I'll fix my own transport."

Webber gave him directions how to get to the house. "You could bring the relevant material at the same time. I'm sure we'll come to some arrangement acceptable to the both of us."

"Let's come to the arrangement first," said James.

"What guarantee will I have?"

"Guys in your bind don't get guarantees."

A pause. "Very well," said Webber.

"There is one thing you might do for me," said James. "I'm running short on cash."

"I might have guessed you'd suggest something like that. An advance payment. Is that it?

"Call it reimbursement of expenses," said James. "An airplane ticket, hotel, transport, walking around money. It mounts up. Say another five thousand dollars?"

"Providing we can work something out I'll give you a cheque."

"Cash would be better."

"That might be a little difficult at such short notices."

"I'm sure you'll think of something," said James.

As soon as he hung up, he called Mustapha's company and asked them to get Mustapha to pick him up at the hotel just as soon as possible. He might smell bad, but James figured as long as the cabby was being well paid, he could be trusted to do what he was told.

"I thought we was through," Mustapha said, as he pulled up outside the hotel and James climbed in back of the cab.

"I need you this afternoon. Okay?"

"Same rate as last time?"

Why not, thought James. He was on his way to pick up five grand.

"You got it," he said.

"Where are we going?"

"Easthampton."

"Hey man! That's out on Long Island. I don't hack out there."

It seemed that Mustapha did not like leaving the island of Manhattan. It made him feel like a foreigner. However, if James wanted to up the ante, say to seventy-five an hour, he might consider it. James couldn't be bothered to argue.

"What are you 'doin out there anyway?" Mustapha wanted to know as they were crossing the Queensboro bridge.

"I want to see how the other half lives," said James. In fact, he'd started to wonder himself what he was 'doin' out here. Hitting Webber for five grand had been too easy. He hadn't felt a thing. Maybe Gary had been wrong when he said James wasn't into blackmail. Just to cover expenses, horseshit! Greedy, avaricious bastard was more like it. Greedy, *unscrupulous*, avaricious bastard. Here he was getting money from a guy to keep quiet about information he didn't even have. That was sinking pretty low, even in his book, which wasn't renowned for the quality of its idealism. Maybe he should do everyone a big favor and forget the whole thing, hop the next airplane home. Don't bother even going back to the hotel. Have Mustapha drop him off at Kennedy here and now, before he changed his mind.

"How long before we get to Kennedy airport?" he said.

"We don't," said Mustapha.

The decision had been made for him. He'd go out to Easthampton, listen to what Jackson Webber had to say, maybe finally get to make some sense out of the whole mess, which wasn't any of his business anyway and never had been. Two people killed and h was chasing around New York trying to find the killer. Mr. Nice Guy. Shit, the cops weren't worried about, why should he be? Maybe he'd take the money. Webber could certainly afford it. On the other hand, maybe, he'd tell Webber to stick it up his ass. He settled back in the seat, adjusting this backside to the broken springs. He told Mustapha to wake him when they reached Easthampton. He was asleep in three minutes flat. Self-doubts had never caused him to lose any sleep.

He didn't wake up until they'd reached Southampton and Mustapha announced that he was lost. They stopped at a gas station where they bought a local map. Ten minutes later, they reached Easthampton and started to look for the Webber House.

It wasn't difficult to find. It was one of five on a curving street running parallel to the beach, just over three quarters of a mile long, which gave each property a road frontage of around two hundred and fifty yards, with a similar stretch of beach at the rear. Highly desirable real estate. The only sign that there was anything lurking behind the highwalls and trees edging the road was an occasional set of gates, some of which were flanked by a gatehouse large enough to accommodate a family of four. No street numbers here, just names. Not of the house, but of the family who owned it. The gates that guarded the Webber property were firmly closed, with no sign of anybody around to open them.

"What happens now?" Mustapha asked.

James got out of the cab and went over to a panel set in the stone work of one of the gateposts. He pressed a button and a moment later a disembodied voice asked him to identify himself.

"James Reed to see Mr. Webber."

Almost immediately the gates started to swing open. James climbed back in the cab and they drove through. The drive curved away to the right, leading to the front of the house, which looked as if it might have been shipped from England brick by brick, two hundred odd years ago. Leaded windows, rich red brick walls, wood beams and trusses, stately chimney stacks, dark slated room and a tower to one side complete with the odd gargoyle or two peering down from the edge.

"Jesus H. Christ!" was Mustapha's reaction. "You figure anyone will give a shit if I wandered around? I ain't never seen a place like this outside of a horror movie."

"Suit yourself," said James. "Just be sure you're here if I need you."

Mustapha looked at him suspiciously. "You ain't expecting trouble? I'm askin' 'cause when I said I could round up some the brothers to break heads, I didn't reckon on being way to hell and gone. The brothers are thin on the ground round these parts."

"I don't think I'm going to need heads broken," said James.

The front door was opened before he reached it by a Filipino houseboy, who bowed low, indicating that James should come in. The entrance hall was in keeping with the outside of the house, paneled with a wide staircase leading to a second-floor landing. James didn't know much about paintings, but he guessed the ones hanging in the hall and on the staircase would have been welcome additions to any self-respecting museum. Doors were open wide to a living room. The windows on the far side gave onto the ornate garden, the pool and tennis court, with the ocean beyond. Four people were on the tennis court and he could see at least three more around the pool. The houseboy led him across the hallway to a pair of double doors, where he knocked and was told to "enter". He stood aside and James walked into the library, where Jackson Webber was waiting.

Webber was exactly as James imagined he would be. Around sixty-three, a shade under six feet tall, well-built, tanned, and with a full head of the kind of white hair that only seems to grow on distinguished Americans. He was standing with his back to the fireplace, beneath an oil painting of an ancestor, so similar in appearance, he could have posed for it himself. He must have changed his clothes since coming off the golf course because was dressed for the office in a dark suit and a discreetly striped shirt and tie. He looked as if he was waiting to be asked to appear on the font cover of *Time* magazine. Although James was probably an inch taller, Webber managed to give the impression he was looking down on his visitor. He didn't offer to shake hands.

"Sit down, Mr. Reed."

James took the indicated chair as Webber walked to the other side of the one of the largest desks James had ever seen. As Webber sat, he seemed to gain a couple of inches in height. James decided that the desk chair must be on a platform. A great idea if you needed to intimidate your visitors except, as far as James was concerned, it was a lost cause.

The whole place had pushed long forgotten buttons connected to his English, working class background, where the upper classes were all supposed to live in grand houses and spend their lives patronizing the less fortunate. He'd long ago insulated himself against such intimidation.

"Good of you to make the journey," said Webber. He obviously hated James's guts, but good breeding won out.

"No problem," said James.

"Would you care for something. Coffee, tea, a drink?" His finger hovered over a bell on his desk.

James said he didn't care for anything right now, thank you very much.

There was a long silence. If Webber expected James to start the proceedings, they were in for a long wait.

"So, Mr. Reed," said Webber, finally.

James gave him no help at all.

Another silence, before Webber decided he would have to take the plunge. "How much are you going to demand for the evidence you have?"

"How much do you consider it worth?"

"Please don't prevaricate. A hundred thousand? Two? A quarter of a million?"

Right now, his problem was finding out what it was he was supposed have for sale. If Webber had reached a quarter of a million without prompting, it had to be worth a hell of a lot more than that to him.

"I was thinking in the region of two million," said James.

To his credit, Webber didn't bat and eyelid. "I'm afraid that's quite out of the question. I can go as high as five hundred thousand dollars. And before you say anything, let me assure you, that is my absolute top limit. If it's not acceptable, then go ahead and publish your filth. In spite of what it will mean to my family and to my social standing. I'm prepared to accept the consequences of my folly."

Okay, thought James, beginning to get the drift, we're not dealing with corruption in high places, we're dealing with personal problems. Tax evasion, maybe. "The authorities are getting pretty touch these days," he said, dangling his hook in the water.

"About what?"

Eighty-six the tax evasion theory. "After all, it's against the law."

"What is? What are you talking about, Mr. Reed?"

Wrong again. He hadn't broken the law. So, it must be personal. And if it was personal it probably had something to do with sex. What the hell could he have done that he was willing to pay half a million dollars to keep quiet about. Maybe he'd screwed the wife of some big wheel who could have his hide nailed to the Stock Exchange door or hung drawn and quartered on the steps of the Met. Webber was looking at him, waiting for an answer.

"Against the law of morality, Mr. Webber."

Webber almost managed a grim little smile. "A blackmailer who is also a puritan. How original."

And suddenly James knew. Maybe it was the way Webber had cocked his head slightly as he looked at James. But whatever it was, he had no doubt. Webber was gay. It figured. A married man with grown up children, on the board of half a dozen charities, a doyen of the business community, possibly looking to go into politics. Half-a-million wasn't too much to enable him to remain deep in the closet. James wondered briefly what Megan had collected on him. Photographs, probably. Suddenly he felt sorry for the man sitting across from him. The only thing he'd done wrong was to employ over enthusiastic helpers. The hell with the money. He'd take the guy off the hook.

"Maybe I will have a drink after all," he said.

For one moment, it looked as if Webber might tell James to take a running jump, but perfect manners prevailed. He rang for the houseboy and told him to fetch the Scotch that James asked for while he'd settle for a Perrier with a slice of lemon. They awaited the arrival of their drinks in total silence. Okay, so he was going to let Webber off the hook, but he was so bloody superior it wouldn't do him any harm to sweat for a few minutes longer. The drinks arrived and the houseboy left, closing the door behind him.

"Cheers!" said James.

Webber took a sip of his drink without responding to the toast. Then he sat back while James told him what was happening. He was a good listener. He didn't interrupt once, saving his questions until James had finished.

"So, you don't have any information on me?"

"None."

"You have no idea why I am vulnerable?"

"I didn't say that."

"But you don't have any evidence."

"None."

"And you don't intend asking me for money."

"No."

"So, what has been the object of this charade?"

"I thought you were responsible for a couple of killings. I figured you were due for some pretty heavy come-uppance."

"So, you have no idea where the locker is located."

"All I know is that it's not in New York. I have the only key, so you can stop worrying over what's in it. Nobody's going to lay their hands on it."

"What do you think is in it, Mr. Reed?"

"Photographs, probably."

"Right. Photographs." He got up from behind the desk and walked to the window. He stared out for a time, before turning back into the room. "Megan worked for me. I met her through her ex-husband. It was through her that I met Paul Menzies. Did you ever meet Paul, Mr. Reed?"

Christ, thought James. He's telling me he went to bed with Paul. "I met him a couple of times."

"We had a short … fling. I suppose you'd call it. The first and only time I ever succumbed to those particular … urges." James doubted that, but he didn't say anything. "Anyway, photographs were taken. Later demands were made."

"By Megan McCoy?"

"Megan made the demands, yes."

Wonderful, thought James. Megan tells her boyfriend to hop into the sack with her boss and they've got a meal ticket for life. "Is that why she was killed?"

"I have no idea why she was killed, or by whom."

"My money was on those two thugs you sent out there. Where did you find those guys anyway?"

"Believe it or not, through Paul. Apparently, he used to attend a health club or gym where those men congregated. When I started looking for Paul, I met this man Gary Bright. He said he could help me find Paul and Megan and get back the photographs. But, like you, I don't think they killed Megan. They had no cause."

"So who did?"

"As I said before. I have no idea."

"How about Paul. Who killed him?" James asked, though he was pretty sure Paul was very much alive.

"Again, I have no idea. I didn't even know he was dead until you told me on the phone. How did it happen?"

"You instructed a man name Bill Goodge to take care of him."

"I told a man named Bill Goodge to try to find him, yes. But that's all."

"Find him for what reason?"

"I wanted to hear the truth, from him. Was he part of the whole scheme from the beginning or was he an innocent participant?" Webber thought about what he'd just said, then he shook his head. "Self-deception is so simple. But, Paul always seemed so ..."

"Good natured," said James, helping him out.

"Good natured. Amiable. Trustworthy."

"I know what you mean," said James. He was in the middle of telling Webber how he'd come to New York with a half-baked, ill-formed notion of avenging good natured, amiable Paul's murder when the door to the library opened and a young girl dress in tennis clothes came in.

"Sorry daddy. I didn't know you were busy." She smiled at James. "Hello. I'm Diana Webber."

She was exactly the type of girl that James used to fall in love with when he was young and still possessed the ability to fall in love. Just being in the same room with her made him feel ancient.

"This is James Reed," said Webber. "A business associate from California."

She was polite enough to pretend there was nothing wrong with his face.

"Where in California?"

"Malibu. That's near L.A."

"I know Malibu. Are you on the beach?"

"Smack bang."

"How super. Next time I'm in Los Angeles, perhaps you'll invite me over for the day." She turned to her father. "There's a black man wandering around the garden, daddy. He says he's a cab driver. We were wondering if we should do anything about him."

"He belongs to me," said James quickly, before Webber could phone someplace to have Mustapha lynched. "He drove me out from New York."

"That's all right then," said Diana. She flashed her beautiful teeth at James. "Nice to have met you, Mr. Reed." She was gone with a swirl of her short tennis skirt, long brown legs, a flash of white panties, leaving behind an aura of youth and nostalgia.

"You were saying, Mr. Reed…?" said Webber, dragging James back to earth.

"I'd finished," said James, who suddenly felt very tired. "I think I'll go back to New York."

"And then?"

"I'm supposed to be going out to the country for the weekend. I'll give it some thought. See how I feel Monday."

"Perhaps this will help you make up your mind," said Webber. He pulled open the desk drawer and flipped an envelope towards James. It held fifty, one hundred dollar bills.

"What's this for?"

"Five thousand dollars, you said. To cover expenses."

"That's when I wanted to give you a hard time," said James. "I've changed my mind." He held out the envelope towards Webber.

"Keep it," said Webber.

"Why?"

"For not giving me a hard time."

What the hell? He'd been prepared to pay $500,000. James slipped the envelope into his pocket.

"What are you going to do with the key?" asked Webber.

"I'll mail it to you before I leave New York."

"The real one this time," he said with the trace of a smile.

"Guaranteed," said James. He stood up, and Webber walked with him to the library door. As they came into the hall, a handsome woman in her middle fifties was doming downstairs. He looked elegant and as hard as nails. Webber introduced her. "My wife, Sunny. This is James Reed, my dear."

"How do you do, Mr. Reed. We spoke on the phone didn't we." Her voice still sounded as if she had sinus problems, but it wasn't quite as obvious as it had been over the telephone. James tried to make the right social noises, whilst Sunny Webber examined him minutely with her ice blue eyes. She took in his damaged face, but what she said was:

"You have an English accent, Mr. Reed."

"That's where I'm from, originally."

"Will you be staying for dinner?"

"Thank you, but I have to be getting back to New York."

"What a pity," she said, without meaning it. Then, with a flash of immaculate teeth, and expensive perfume, she was gone. One very tough lady, decided James. The kind of lady who, on discovering that her husband was gay, might take a pair of cutting shears to his personal equipment. If he'd been in Webber's shoes, he too would have been prepared to cough up a few hundred grand to keep her ignorant.

Webber walked him out to where Mustapha was waiting behind the wheel of his cab. As soon as he saw Webber, Mustapha got out and opened the rear door for James. It was the kind of thing that must happen for Jackson Webber all the time. Waiters doormen, cab drivers, there was something about Webber that commanded respect and deference without him having to do or say anything.

He shook hands with James. "If you decide to stay on in New York and you need anything, don't hesitate to call me. Good bye, Mr. Reed." He turned and walked back into the house.

"Pretty high-class people you know," said Mustapha, as they were waiting for the gates to open. "I walked round back and there they all was, half-a-dozen or them, and none of them batted an eyelid. Then this pretty little gal, she asks me polite like, if there is anything, she can do to help me. Shit man, if I'd've wandered into some honky backyard in Queens, they'd have shot me first, then done the askin'."

James wasn't much in the mood for conversation. Right now, he had some heavy decisions to make. He told Mustapha to shut up and just drive.

"So, where you wanna go?"

Then he decided the hell with the decisions. They could wait until Monday. He was going away for the weekend with a sexy lady. He told Mustapha to drive back into Manhattan, wait for him at the hotel while he threw some stuff into a bag, then take him on to Wanda's apartment.

It took him three minutes to pack. Downstairs, he told the front desk that he'd be out-of-town for the weekend but he'd keep his room on. He left the envelope Webber had given him in the safe, along with the locker key, then he turned his bag over to Mustapha who was parked outside. He went to the nearest liquor store on Third avenue. There he bought two bottles of champagne and a small pot of Beluga caviar.

"Hot weekend?" Mustapha asked.

"I sincerely hope so," said James.

They drove to Wanda's place where James settled up with Mustapha. Five hours at $75 per.

"Maybe you should buy the cab," said Mustapha.

"I already did, twice over," said James. "I'll probably be needing you Monday. I'll give you a call."

James asked the doorman to call 1407 and inform Mr. Francis that he was waiting downstairs and please remind her to not forget her electric toothbrush. He was told that she would be down in five minutes. Fifteen minutes later, she appeared with Prune in tow and ten minutes after that he was sitting in the passenger seat beside her, with Prune on his lap, and they were on the Henry Hudson Parkway, heading for Lake Waramaug, Connecticut.

Wanda had been suitably distressed when she'd first seen the state of his face. Now she wanted to know exactly what was going on, I mean, here they were, going away for the weekend together and she knew next to nothing about him except that he lived in California and knew some very strange people in New York. James stopped her asking questions by telling her it would be safer if she didn't know anything because then the men that did this to him wouldn't bother her again. She accepted what he said, but James could tell it was only temporary. Later, he was going to have to come up with some kind of explanation. Until then, lay back and enjoy.

An hour and forty minutes after leaving Manhattan, they reached New Preston. Two minutes later, they were skirting the edge of

Lake Waramaug. The sun was starting to dip, across the far side of the lake, throwing the opposite bank into deep shadow. A couple of small sail boats were stranded mid-lake for lack of wind, while a dinghy with an outboard motor cut a white swathe across the flat blue green of the water. It was a million miles from New York. Halfway around the lake, Wanda pointed out Boulder Inn as a place where they could have dinner unless he wanted her to cook again, in which case they'd need to go to the store. He made her pull in and wait when he went inside and reserved a table for eight thirty.

Wanda's house was a converted barn on the edge of the lake. It was built on the grounds of a large house which, she told him, belonged to a family who lived in Philadelphia and who rarely ever used the place. They were distantly related to friend Lonnie and had been happy to grant a long-term lease of the barn to her and Wanda. The girls had an arrangement with a local woman, who they phoned when they were going to drive up and she would open the place, air it and put enough food in the icebox to get them through their first breakfast. The first floor consisted of a large living room with a kitchen area at one end and an open wood burning fireplace at the other. Upstairs, there were two bedrooms with a bathroom between. It was decorated in a style James labelled "Bloomingdale country casual." But he made the right noises of appreciation as she showed him around. He wanted to drag her into bed right away, but she had other ideas. She put the champagne in the ice box and told James to take Prune for a walk around the garden while she had a bath. Okay, he could handle clean. Twenty minutes later, he was back and raring to go, maybe he'd even surprise her in the tub and they could slosh around in the soapy water. But she was out of tub wearing a shapeless tracksuit, busy watering the house plants. After the plants, she quickly vacuumed the living room in case the cleaning woman had missed anything. Then she announced the hot water had replenished itself sufficiently for James to take his bath. She was wrong, but he climbed in the tub anyway. There didn't seem any other place left to go. By the time, he was dressed again, she was wearing something 'country casual' and the champagne was cold enough not to give offense. He had just started to feel good again when she led him out to the boathouse and showed him the small dinghy with an outboard motor. This was how they were going to Boulder Inn for dinner.

"Can't we take the car?" He disliked boats intensely.

"We always use the dinghy," said Wanda. Her attitude had changed gears slightly. Maybe it was the country air, or maybe she'd made a decision already about him.

She showed him how to start the outboard motor, and they travelled across the lake to tie up at the landing of Boulder Inn, where they were just in time for their dinner reservation. She told him she ate here often and maybe it wouldn't be a bad idea if she ordered the meal. And as he already knew she was a wine expert, she'd order that too. A couple hours and $150 later, they chugged back across the lake in the dark, guided by the lights Wanda had left on in the house. By the time he tied up the dinghy, walked Prune around the garden and locked up, she was already in bed. They made love with an easy familiarity, as though they had been doing it together for years. It was a lot less exciting than last time. Sunday, she told him to drive to the village store where he could buy the *New York Times*, which they read all over the living room floor while they drank the second bottle of champagne and ate the caviar. They went to bed and made love again in the afternoon.

Then she said it might be a nice idea to have supper at home tonight, so he got up and went to the store again and bought steaks, which he cooked while she gave Prune a bath and dried him with her blow dryer. After supper, she suggested he walk Prune again while she did the dishes. Later, there was something she wanted to watch on television. When the program was over, she woke him up to tell him it was bedtime. They didn't make love. Sometime in the night, he must have started to snore, because when he woke up in the middle of the night to go to the bathroom, she was gone from the bed. She was sleeping in the other bedroom, Prune at her feet. Neither of them opened their eyes as he looked in on them.

At six a.m. the alarm woke him. He was feeling a little horny so he went next door and tried to get in bed with her. She looked at the clock and said there wasn't time. By seven, he'd walked Prune, made the coffee, squeezed the juice, measured out the cereal and burned the toast, which she didn't want anyway because she'd taken so long getting dressed that they had to leave right away or she'd be late for work and would he drive because she wanted to do her nails in the car because she hadn't be able to do them over the weekend what with how busy they'd been having such a wonderful time and perhaps he could drive her straight to the office then take the car back to the apartment, unload it, give Prune a tiny walk, take her upstairs, put out her food, switch on the air conditioning then leave the keys with the guy at the desk on his way out and she'd see him for dinner this evening when they'd go to this new place on Amsterdam she'd been wanting to try, unless he like to eat at home in which case the Food Emporium would stock everything he might need, but for real gourmet value he should go to Zabar's which was a few blocks north but well worth it.

On the road, ten minutes later, he said he couldn't be sure about dinner, he didn't know where he'd be. She started to sulk and only cheered up when he said he'd call her at the office just as soon as he had his day worked out. For the first time in his life, James was glad to see the spires of New York city.

SEVEN

He called Patsy McCoy's number from Wanda's apartment. Patsy answered the phone. He hung up immediately. She was home at last. He called the cab company and asked them to find Mustapha Zee and have him pick him up at the apartment building as soon as he could make it. Ten minutes later they phoned from downstairs to tell him his cab had arrived. He said goodbye to Prune, locked up and left he keys with the guys at the desk.

"Is this going to be on the clock?" Mustapha wanted to know before James had even settled back.

"I'll tell you in about fifteen minutes," said James. He told Mustapha to take him to the address McCoy had given him for Patsy. Mustapha took off down Broadway. He didn't smell quite so bad this morning, maybe he took a bath on the weekend. After a couple of blocks, he stared to get chatty.

"How about them motherfuckers," he said.

"Which motherfuckers?"

"Them South Africans, I saw on the TV last night, they got a heap of them over there in Africa look just like them Nazis used to, with swastikas and burning flags and heiling and all that shit."

"They're dangerous people," said James gravely.

"So, what's happening today, man? We gonna be breakin' any heads, stuff like that?"

"Surveillance," said James. He refused to say any more on the grounds that Mustapha didn't have a security clearance.

✤ ✤ ✤

The address was on Fifth Avenue between 8th and 9th Street just north of Washington Square, a large unattractive apartment building. Having located the building, James told Mustapha to find the nearest pay phone.

"What's a matter? You gone blind." There was a pay phone on the sidewalk right out front of the main entrance to the building.

"I didn't see it," said James.

"No wonder the country's up the creek with guys like you taking care of security and stuff," said Mustapha.

James went to the pay phone where he dialed Patsy McCoy again.

"Hi! This is James Reed," he said when she answered.

"I'm sorry. Do I know you?"

"Malibu. Remember?"

"Of course, Mr. Reed. A friend of my stepmother. It must be the middle of the night out there."

"It's pretty early in the a.m., I must admit. But I'm an early riser. I wondered if you could help me with something. I'm trying to find Paul Menzies." There was a silence on the other end of the line. "Hello?"

"I'm still here," said Patsy. "What do you want with Paul?"

"I have something that belongs to him."

"Something of Megan's?" There was an edge of excitement in her voice.

"I'm sorry, Ms. McCoy. I can't tell you that. Only Paul."

There was another silence as she considered the permutations. "I thought you knew, Paul's dead."

"Well, actually he's not," said James.

"I don't understand."

"He's not dead. People just think he is."

"What a strange thing to say."

"It's a strange would we live in," said James. "I'm sorry to have troubled you." He hung up before she could say anything else.

He walked back to where Mustapha was parked, twenty-five yards past the entrance to the building. He debated whether or not to get in the cab but decided against it. Instead, he leaned up against it looking towards the apartment building.

"What happens now?" Mustapha wanted to know from behind the wheel.

"Now we wait?"

"Waiting costs money, man."

"The clock is running."

"Come on. Make a deal or I'm out of here. Same rate as before. Seventy-five per hour."

It was already getting hot. There was a good chance that this would turn out to be one very shitty day. James decided to conserve his energies by not arguing.

"Okay," he said.

He'd estimated that as soon as he hung up on her she'd try to call him back at the only number she had for him, the beach house. When there was no answer, she'd have some heavy thinking to do. Maybe a couple more phone calls. Then hopefully, she'd put in an appearance.

"Maybe she won't show," Mustapha after twenty-five minutes.

"Maybe you're right," said James.

At that moment, Patsy McCoy came out of the building and turned right, in the opposite direction of where James was waiting. James took off after her. Mustapha started his engine and took off after James, keeping a respectful distance.

Patsy was wearing a light summer frock with a full skirt and flat shoes. She looked about sixteen. At the corner of the block, she turned right and disappeared. By the time James reached the corner and looked down the street, she was unlocking the door of a small red compact. James waved to Mustapha. By the time

Patsy pulled out, James was back in the cab and they were right behind her.

She took the Holland Tunnel to Jersey City, which immediately made Mustapha nervous. He reminded James he didn't like getting off the island of Manhattan. When they reached the New Jersey Turnpike, she headed South.

"She's goin' to the airport," said Mustapha.

"I don't think so," said James.

He was right. She continued on past Newark airport.

"I'm gonna runout of gas in about twenty more miles," said Mustapha as they transferred to the Garden State Parkway. He didn't make it. He ran out of gas in fifteen. They coasted to the side of the highway and James watched Patsy's compact disappear fast.

"What kind of a cab driver are you anyway?" he asked.

Mustapha flashed his teeth. "With the money you're paying me, man, a rich one."

Twenty minutes, later, a tow truck, summoned by Mustapha over the highway emergency phone, brought them a can of gas, sufficient to drive to the service station, where James bought himself a local road map. They'd been traveling south towards Atlantic City. James examined the route ahead, wondering where in the hell Patsy could be heading, and not holding out much hope of guessing. He was wrong. He spotted it almost immediately. Spring Lake was twenty-five minutes further south and a couple of miles off the Parkway.

"The McCoys own a summer place in Spring Lake, I used to keep my eye on it," Paul Menzies had told him.

James walked back to where Mustapha had just finished gassing up.

"All set?" he asked.

"Soon as you pay the man," said Mustapha.

James paid for the gas plus another $50 to cover the tow truck's ride out to the Parkway.

"Back to New York, right?" said Mustapha.

"Spring Lake," said James.

"Never heard of it. Listen, man. Get yourself another driver. I'm getting my ass on back to the city."

"Suit yourself," said James. "But you don't get paid."

Mustapha thought about it for a few seconds. "Okay, motherfucker. Get in."

James got in and they took off again.

Spring Lake looked as if it had been caught in a time warp. Elegant old wood frame houses set in their own grounds, screened by trees and hedges; two miles of beach which required a permit to get onto; a lake, set in an immaculately kept park with a rustic bridge and a couple of three shaded tennis courts; a small main street, almost devoid of traffic. The whole place had a rather dusty air of faded elegance. James had Mustapha drive around for about five minutes before ordering him to pull over at a pay phone. There, he looked up the name McCoy in the local phone book. It was there, complete with address. A middle-aged couple were walking an elderly dog. James asked them if they knew the address he was looking for. They both knew it and they both had different ideas as to the best way to get there. They were still arguing with each other when James rejoined Mustapha and told him to drive three blocks, hang a left, two more blocks, hang a right and stop.

He told Mustapha to wait. He got out of the cab and walked the remainder of the block and turned left. The house he was looking for was the third one down. It was screened from the road by hedges and trees. As James walked past the main entrance, he could see the curve of the drive, with the tennis court on the left. The garage was next to it, adjoining the main house. Wide enough for three cars, with a couple of rooms built over. Patsy's car was parked out front. James walked back to where he'd left Mustapha.

"Okay. I'm not gonna need you for a while. You can take off for a couple of hours."

"What the fuck am I supposed to do?"

"Whatever you like. I'll see you back here in two hours. If I'm not here, wait for another two. If I haven't shown by then, go to the police."

"Sure you don't want me to call Washington D.C. You bein' in the CIA and all."

"The police will do fine."

"Sure they will 'cause the CIA ain't never heard of you. Right, man? You've gotta think I'm some kinda lunkhead tryin' that shit on me. I knew you weren't CIA right from the start."

"It kept you around."

"You know what kept me around? Findin' some honky asshole dumb enough to pay me seventy-five an hour for doin' a job I'd've done for twenty. That's what kept me around. So, what do you want I should tell the police when you don't show?"

"That I'm probably dead."

"Best news I heard all day," said Mustapha.

James walked back past the McCoy house. There was no sign of occupation other than the car. A few yards past the entrance, he stopped. He had a quick look up and down the street before preparing to climb the low wall. Half a block further down the street, on the next property an old guy wearing a battered, straw hat was trimming his front hedge, trying to look like he was taking no notice of what was happening next door. James changed his mind. Instead of climbing the wall, he started towards the old guy whose concentration on his hedge cutting immediately became total. This was definitely the kind of neighborhood where people pretended to mid nobody's business but their own and unless James had it figured all wrong, this was the kind of guy who knew everything about everybody.

"Good Morning," said James, in his most burnished British accent. "I wonder if you could possibly assist me?"

The man looked at him from red rimmed, rheumy eye. He was about seventy-five years old with a stubble of white bristles and badly fitting dentures. "Depends," he said.

James took out his wallet and flashed it. It still held his Metropolitan Police ID. Years out of date. It would never fool anybody in authority, but it had proved useful cashing the occasional check, getting in to see a Lakers game or sweet talking his way out of a traffic violation.

"New Scotland Yard," said James, in case the old guy's eyes weren't too good.

He pretended he wasn't impressed. "That's London, England. Right?"

"Right," said James. He looked up and down the street before continuing. "I'm here on a surveillance mission and I need your help Mister …?"

"Fogerty, Harold P. What are you surveying?"

"The house next door."

"The McCoy's place? What's he been up to?"

"Mr. McCoy's in the clear, but we have reason to believe the house is being used for illegal purposes."

"What illegal purposes?"

"Believe me, Mr. Fogerty. You wouldn't want to know."

"Yes, I would," said Fogerty, flatly.

"Drugs."

"Ah!" Fogerty nodded his head a couple of times. "So?"

"I wondered if you'd noticed anything about the place over the past few days."

"Yep!"

"Yep, what?"

"Yep. I noticed something."

This was getting to be hard work. "What did you notice?"

"Somebody's shacked up in there. I been watching the place on and off. See, I know Mr. McCoy ain't using it right now and I wondered who it was."

"You've seen him?"

"Sure have. I seen him comin' and goin' at night."

"Going where?"

"Jogging. Regular as clockwork. Midnight to three a.m. See, I don't sleep much these days. I reckon when you're as old as me, it's a waste of time sleeping. So, I'm up most nights, fixin' things around the house. He takes off up the service street at back like the hounds of hell were on his heels. Comes back the same way three hours later. Must be the fittest young feller I ever saw."

"Every night?"

"Five out of the past six."

"He may have gone then, too. I just didn't see him. Me and the wife were … you know." Then he shrugged. What the hell! "At least, we were trying. What kind of drugs is he into?"

"Cocaine," said James. "Wholesale only," he added quickly. He didn't want Fogerty banging on the front door asking to borrow a neighborly cup of happy dust.

"So, what you donna do about it?"

"Don't you worry, Mr. Fogerty."

"I'm not worried, young feller. I'm just curious."

"I'll keep in touch," said James.

"You do that," said Fogerty.

Two hours later Patsy McCoy drove off. James, who was sitting on a bench at the edge of the park, pretending to enjoy the sun, watched her go. Then he walked back to the place where he had arranged to meet Mustapha. He was sleeping behind the wheel.

All the windows were closed. It must have been like an oven in there. James banged on the window and Mustapha rolled it down.

"Hey, man! What's happening?"

"Soon as you've aired out the cab, we'll go back to New York."

"Where in New York?"

"The gym on 35th," said James.

"Ain't that where you got beat up?"

"That was last week," said James.

"Shit, man! What you wanna go back there for?"

Mustapha had come this far with him, why not go the whole hog. "I need to buy a handgun," he said.

"You don't need to go back to that place, man. I know a guy who'll fit you out with what you need."

Why not, thought James. No point in getting involved with Gary again. Maybe by now he'd worked out that James had lied to him. Bill *was* dead.

"How much is this going to cost me?"

"The going rate is five hundred bucks and ten bucks each for bullets which means a full house is gonna cost you another eighty."

"You're on," said James. "Get it back to me before midnight."

"Cash in advance," said Mustapha.

James started to count out the money. "How do I know you won't just take the money and pull a no show?"

"You really want to know?"

"That's why I'm asking."

Mustapha checked the money before leaning into the cab, reaching under the glove box and producing a revolver. He handed it to James with a grin. "Service with a smile, man!"

James checked it carefully. It seemed okay. "Is it clean?"

"It ain't got any names attached to it, if that's what you mean," said Mustapha. "I bought it from a guy, who bought it from a guy who knocked over a gun store."

"For five hundred bucks?"

"Are you kidding! I gotta have mark up, man."

"Okay. I guess you can split," said James.

"You don't want me to hang around some more?"

"At seventy-five an hour, you've got to be kidding."

"Where guns are involved, I come more expensive."

"That's what I figured," said James.

"But for you, I'll make an exception."

"You're all heart. But no thanks. Should anyone ever ask, you've never heard of me."

"Who?"

"Exactly." He paid Mustapha what he owed him, including an extra hour to cover the drive back to New York.

"It'll take me more than an hour."

"Drive fast," said James.

Mustapha looked at him a moment, then he grinned and shook his head. "CIA! Shit man!" He climbed behand the wheel, "Y'all take care now," he said. He almost looked as if he meant it.

James walked to the main street section of town. He found a small restaurant where he ordered himself some lunch. After lunch, he found a hardware store where he bought a flashlight and a couple of stout leather straps, the kind used to secure a suitcase when it had been overpacked. Then he went back to the park, chose a shady spot under a tree, laid down and went to sleep. He was awakened two hours later by a couple of dogs sniffing around him while their owner watched from a few feet away wondering whether or not her pets had unearthed a corpse. It was four thirty p.m. What the hell was he going to do with the rest of the day?

He walked along the sea front for an hour. The beach made him nostalgic for Malibu. He went into a large hotel across from the beach, where aged vacationers sat rocking on the long veranda. He spent an hour in the lobby trying to find if there was any part of the *Sunday Times* that he had missed yesterday at Lake Waramaug. At six thirty, he bought a couple of drinks in the hotel bar before walking back into town, finding another restaurant and having some dinner, complete with a bottle of wine. So now it was nine p.m. He had another three hours to kill. He walked around the park a couple of times, counting fireflies. He bought himself another drink at a hotel bar, counted some more fireflies, checked out a third hotel where they featured live music played by a bunch of middle-aged guys in old fashioned tuxedos, watched the kids coming out of the movie theater, then he had one more drink before heading back towards the McCoy place. The town was about to go to bed and his day was just starting.

He found a hiding place in a neighboring back yard, behind somebody's garage, among their garbage cans. From there, he could look down the narrow street at back of the McCoy property. There was an overhead light about halfway down the street, another at the far end. The rest was in darkness. A nervous dog, out for his last pee, sensed, rather than saw James. He barked a couple of times, just to stake out his territorial rights, then grew bored and went back indoors. A prowling cat arrived to inspect the garbage cans and nearly had a coronary when James shooed it off. He checked the gun for the third time, transferring it from pocket to the waistband of his pants. He had an urge to take a pee, which he did up against the side of the garage, trying to do it quietly. It was twenty minutes to midnight and even the fireflies had gone to bed. Maybe he wouldn't show tonight. Maybe Patsy's visit had exhausted his energies. Maybe Fogerty didn't know what he was talking about. Then, exactly at midnight, James heard the creak of the back gate. A moment later he saw a shadowy figure emerge and start briskly down the street towards where he was hiding. He ducked back into the shadow, but not before he had definitely identified Paul Menzies.

Getting into the house didn't prove much of a problem. He let himself in through the back gate, from where Paul had emerged. From there, he could just see the pool with a gazebo at the back and what looked like a formal rose garden separating it from the house. Whatever McCoy did for City Hall, it sure paid well. The house itself looked deserted. No lights, shutters closed over all the windows.

When he reached the house, he tried peering through one of the shutters, but all he could see by the light of the street lamps was that the drapes were drawn inside the house. He moved along the side towards the front. Same here, shutters over all the windows and drapes drawn on the inside. He chose a window which looked as though it might open into a store room or downstairs bathroom. He broke off a short length of twig from a convenient shrub, which he used to probe between the shutters until he located the hook that held them together. In a moment, the shutters were open and he was confronted by the window containing four panes of frosted glass. He pressed his ear against the glass. He could hear nothing. But then he didn't expect Paul was sharing the accommodations with anybody or he wouldn't be breaking and entering in the middle of the night. He turned his back to the window and drove his elbow hard at one of the lower panes. The glass was thicker than he'd thought. It broke, but for a moment he thought he might have fractured his elbow. He removed most of the broken glass from the frame, reached inside and unlatched the window. Obviously, security wasn't a major problem her in Spring Lake.

Climbing in wasn't easy due to the fact the window was four feet from the ground and not particularly wide. He ended up wriggling through, finishing up on the floor. He was in what the real estate agents delight in calling 'half a bathroom' in that there was a WC and handbasin. The door leading to heaven knows where, was shut. Again, James had a good listen before making a move, pressing this ear against the door panel. Nothing. Not a sound, other than the rapid thumping of his own heart trying to cope with all the extra adrenalin that he was pumping out.

He turned the handle slowly and pulled the door open a fraction. The hall beyond was in almost total darkness, so he used his flashlight for the first time to establish the geography. The bathroom where he was standing was located at the opposite end of the hall to the front door. There was a faint small of fresh perked coffee in the air. Still he could hear anything. After a moment, he pushed the door wide and moved into the hall. The furniture was old and of good quality. To the left, double doors led to the living room. Opposite was the dining room, with a kitchen beyond. A coat stand near the front door held umbrellas, walking sticks, two polo mallets and an old baseball bat. If Paul was using the kitchen, he was being very tidy about it. Nothing was out of place. Everything spotless.

Upstairs he went through the bedrooms quickly, looking for the one that Paul might be using. He found it at the back, the smallest room in the house, spartan in its furnishings. A table and chair, a bed, a dresser and a small built-in closet. An equally unimpressive bathroom led off, leading in turn to another small bedroom which James worked out was built over the garage. These were obviously designed as the staff quarters. There was very little in the way of personal possessions. A couple of shirts and a pair of running shoes. Add this lot to what he was wearing the Paul cold put all his worldly goods in a large paper bag.

He went through everything carefully, not sure what he was looking for and finding nothing. It was twelve fifteen. If Fogerty was right, and Paul stayed true to form, he now had two- and three-quarter hours more to wait. He chose the bedroom at the opposite end of the passage to the one Paul was using. If he left the door ajar and moved the wingback chair slightly, he could sit and keep his eye on the top of the stairs, the whole of the passage and Paul's room at the end. This way he'd be in total control of any situation, choosing exactly the right moment to make his sudden appearance. Unfortunately, five minutes after he sat down, he fell asleep.

Paul Menzies might have been a very large young man, but he moved very quietly. The first James was aware he'd returned was when a light went on. He came out of a sleep without any idea where he was or what he was doing, just as Paul quietly closed his bedroom door at the end of the passage. Shit! He'd lost the best part of his edge: the ability to know exactly where Paul was and what he was doing. For all he knew, Paul could be in the bedroom, the bathroom, or the bedroom beyond, which James now felt sure, led down to the garage. A cock up of the first magnitude. Still, there was nothing he could do about it. He checked the gun again for the tenth time, got to his feet and started along the passage, keeping his eye on the strip of light under Paul's door. A board squeaked under his foot and he froze, wondering for a brief second how come it hadn't squeaked when Paul stepped on it. He realized it probably had and he'd slept through it. Thank Christ he didn't snore.

After a moment he moved again, keeping his fingers crossed he didn't hit any more ill-fitting floor boards. He reached the door without making any more noise. Silence from the other side. Then he heard it, the sound of a shower being switched on. Hallelujah! He waited a couple of seconds before very carefully turning the door handle and pushing the door open. The door to the bathroom was half open, the light on in there too. He crossed the bedroom in two strides and peered into the bathroom. Paul was in the shower and James was home free. At least he as was as far as this phase of the operation was concerned.

❧ ❧ ❧

When Paul came into the bedroom, toweling himself dry, James was standing on the far side of the bed, waiting. He was holding the gun loosely, half hidden behind his back. "Hi, Paul."

To his credit, Paul didn't go into shock. "Hey! Mr. Reed, I thought you were in L.A."

"Is that what Patsy told you?"

Paul thought about this for a moment. "Dumb broad. You followed her here. Right?"

"You've got it."

He became aware of his nakedness. "Mind if I get some clothes on?"

"Go ahead."

James watched him as he dragged on a pair of shorts and a t-shirt. He really was all muscle. "How'd you get in?"

"It wasn't too difficult."

"I'm only asking, cause if you did any damage, I'll have to fix it. See, I'm minding the place for the McCoys."

"Convenient."

Paul ignored the sarcasm. "Sure is. So how you been?"

"Just fine. Yourself?"

"Okay, I guess. Not much fun being cooped up like this. But you know how it is."

"No, I don't. That's why I'm here. I'd like you to tell me."

"Don't mind me asking, Mr. Reed, but what's it to you?"

"That's a good question. If I come up with an answer, I'll let you know."

Paul thought about things for a moment. "You want something to eat?" he said finally.

"I've eaten."

"I haven't. Come on down to the kitchen. We can talk down there." He crossed to the door and stood aside for James to precede him through.

"You first," said James.

That's when Paul saw the gun. "Hey Mr. Reed. What are you doing with a gun?"

"Nothing. I hope. After you."

Paul led the way out of the bedroom and downstairs. Only when he reached the kitchen did he turn on the light. The drapes were all drawn tight shut. No light would be visible from outside. James sat at the kitchen table while Paul burrowed in the ice box and made himself a sandwich.

"You want a drink?" he asked. "I don't have any liquor, but you can have a diet soda if you want."

James declined. Paul finished making his sandwich, pulled up a hair opposite James and sat down. Just before he started to eat, he nodded at the gun which James was still holding, his hand resting on the table top. "You wouldn't use that, would you Mr. Reed?" It was half question, half statement.

"Let's not even go into it," said James. "So, tell me. What's been happening since you knocked off Bill Goodge?"

"Poor old Bill. I knew him from before, you know. Remember, I told you. Him and Gary, they came down here one time and tried to push me around."

"Webber sent them because you were messing with is lady. Right?"

"There was enough for both of us, for crying out loud. Anyway, I sent 'em packing."

"You're full of shit," said James.

Paul's eyes narrowed fractionally. He didn't look quite so much like the overgrown puppy dog any longer, except maybe one about to develop rabies.

"How come you can say something like that, Mr. Reed? Especially as none of this is any of your business. Hasn't been right from the start."

"I made it my business when I thought you'd been killed."

Paul looked him, disbelieving. "You're kidding!"

"Stupid maybe, but not kidding."

Paul shook his head. "Wow!" He was back to looking like a puppy dog again. "Nobody's ever did anything like that for me. Incidentally, Patsy says you got something of mine."

"That's what I told her."

"Mind telling me what it is?"

"A key," said James.

"Safe deposit … something like that?"

"Something like that."

"You got it from Megan. Right?"

"I don't have it anymore."

A moment's pause. "You don't?"

"I turned it over to Jackson Webber when I went out to see him over the weekend."

Paul said nothing for a long moment. Finally, he stood up and went to the icebox to fetch himself another diet soda. He popped the top as he came back to his seat at the table. "I'll bet he was glad to get it."

"He was."

"You figure I was gonna blackmail him."

"It had crossed my mind."

Paul shook his head. "Not true, Mr. Reed. I'm not into stuff like that. Way back when Megan first told me about, I said to her, no way Jose. I climbed in the sack with him, sure. But heck that's what I do."

"A midnight cowboy."

"Whatever. Guys pay to get laid by me same as chicks. Makes no difference to me either way. A buck's a buck. Shit, if I was into blackmailing everybody I've humped over the past couple years, I'd be a millionaire by now. I could name you names that'd curl your hair, Mr. Reed. Business people, politicians, movie stars even."

"You're into killing people, too."

"Bill Goodge? Poor old Bill. I had to kill Bill or the cops would have been after me forever. I did you a big favor."

"You did?"

"Sure, I did. They closed the book on Megan's case, so you don't have to worry no more."

"Worry about what?"

"Come on, Mr. Reed. We both know you done it. Otherwise why did you go identifying my dead body like that."

"I thought it was you."

"Bullshit. You had to know that was Bill Goodge on that slab with the font of his face all caved in. Shit, you were the one who did it to him."

"They told me a soft drink machine fell on his face."

"Yeah. That was pretty smart of me, 'right?"

"I didn't kill Megan," said James. Somehow it was important that he get that fact across to Paul.

"Whatever," said Paul. He really didn't care one way or the other. "But listen, it's cool. The law thinks Paul Menzies killed Megan and the law thinks Paul Menzies is dead. Case closed. So, I figure you owe me."

Either the kid was a consummate liar, or he was as thick as two planks, James couldn't make up his mind. "What do you figure I owe you Paul?"

"You know me, Mr. Reed. I ain't gonna hold you to nothing. It's just that if you can come up with a few bucks so's I can get out of here and start someplace fresh, that would be a real big help."

"I don't think so."

Paul shrugged. "If you can't, you can't. Patsy says she'll help out. She already has, letting me use this place. But I gotta tell you. I'm going stir crazy."

"How's she going to help out?"

"She says she'll come up with some bread so's we can both split. She figures she's in love with me or something."

"Maybe she's not as high minded as you are. Maybe she's planning on blackmailing Jackson Webber."

Paul shrugged his massive shoulders. "Who knows from chicks."

"What did she tell you about me?"

"You'd called her from L.A. and you had something that belonged to me. I told her to forget it. She came down from New York to talk me around. I guess."

"Did she?"

"Nope. I told her soon as she walked in, she was wasting her time. I tell you, Mr. Reed, when I make up my mind on something, that's it."

"So, what's she going to do now?"

"Search me! Maybe she'll try to hit on you herself. I don't know. All I care about right now is rustling up enough bread to get out from under because as long as I'm shacking her, I have to do pretty much what Patsy tells me. Like right now, it's okay 'cause I'm fucking her regular and she likes that a whole lot. But soon as she gets tired of that, she'll start making demands that maybe I won't be so happy to carry out…like hitting on Mr. Webber with that stuff Megan put together."

"How was she able to do that?"

"Megan! She was working for Webber, like she was his secretary or something. He was banging her on the side until she figured he was getting set to ditch her so she thought she oughta get something on him, kinda like some insurance for her old age. That's when she came to me."

"Why you?"

"She knew me from down here, when I used to take care of this place for them."

"You were screwing her then?"

"Man, I was screwing her from when I was twelve years old. I came to a kid's party, right here in this house. It was Patsy's birthday or something. Megan had just married old man McCoy. I was in the bathroom taking a pee when she came in and locked the door and grabbed me."

"How'd she figure Webber would go for a guy?"

"Shit, man! Who knows? Pillow talk maybe. Anyway, it wasn't strictly just going with a guy, she talked him into a three-some. Him, her and me. Then just when things were getting hot, she hops out of bed and shoots off some happy snaps. After that, things got a bit heavy. She started wanting more and more off me. Webber got pissed off because he was still fucking her himself and sent his goons down here and I said fuck it and I went to California." There was a long silence, broken finally by Paul. "So, what happens now, Mr. Reed?"

"You go to jail," said James.

Paul looked at him for a long moment. "What the fuck for?"

"Killing Megan McCoy."

"Christ man! How many times I gotta tell you? I didn't knock her off. Okay, okay, I pushed her around a bit in the parking lot that night. 'Fact is, she said she was gonna let me have some bread and I'd come up to collect. Then she changed her mind and told me to get lost. All I could see was I was gonna have to walk all the ways back to the beach. Shit man, that's fifteen, twenty miles. I got real pissed off and laid one on her. Then I saw you coming out of the hotel so I split. And that's the honest to God truth."

"Even if I believed you, which I don't. You're still going to jail for killing Bill Goodge."

"Come on! I did everyone a favor."

"So plead extenuating circumstances."

Another silence. Then Paul started to shake his head from side-to-side. "No sir. There's no way I'm going to jail. No way at all. No sir. I'd die in jail Mr. Reed, and that's an absolute, money in the bank, fact. So, you do whatever you think you have to. But don't even think about tryin' to railroad me off to jail 'cause I'm not going." He thought about it for a couple of seconds, then he shook his head again, harder this time. "No sir, I'd die if I had to go to jail."

"Give me an argument and you might die anyway," said James, trying to sound a lot tougher than he felt.

Paul managed a small smile. "No sir, Mr. Reed. Maybe you'd shoot me in the leg or in the arm or something, but you wouldn't kill me less I was trying to kill you. Even then you'd think twice about it. Am I right?"

"You're pushing your luck is what you're doing."

"My luck's due to run out soon anyway, Mr. Reed. All I got going for me is my looks. I'm pushing twenty-eight, man. How much longer am I gonna be able to get by earning a living by fucking people? And before you go tellin' me to learn a trade or get a proper job or something, forget it. I'm not too bright. Never have been since I was a kid. So, the way I figure it. I'm going to walk out of here right now. Either you let me go or you try to stop me and the only way you're going to be able to do that is to use that gun you got here. Maybe you will, maybe you won't and to tell you the honest to God truth, right now I don't much give a fuck either way. I'm going upstairs to throw what I got into a bag and then I'm taking off. Maybe I'll try my luck in Atlantic City for a couple of weeks. Some of those old folks down from New York aren't too fussy who gets their rocks off for them. Get some place like Tahiti or Bali, one of them places that's all beach, where the sun shines all the time and you can live off coconuts and ten cents a week. I've seen places like that in the travel brochures. So, I guess I'll see you around Mr. Reed." He stood up and walked out of the kitchen, leaving James sitting at the table, still holding the gun.

Threatening somebody with a gun is only effective if that person believes you are capable and willing to use it. If he doesn't or if, as in Paul's case, he honestly doesn't care one way or other, then the gun is a useless piece of equipment and James had blown five hundred dollars. He shoved it back in his pocket and tried to figure out his next move. He'd tell the LAPD how he'd made a mistake in the ID and that Paul Menzies was still on the loose.

Let them pick him up. That's it. He'd fly back to LA tomorrow. But let's give the poor, simple-minded kid a fighting chance and let him know what's happening. He got to feet and started out of the kitchen, wondering vaguely how he was going to get back to New York at one o'clock in the morning. As he stepped into the hall some long forgotten instinct screamed a silent warning. He was still reaching for his gun when he was grabbed from behind. Two arms wrapping around him, pinning his own arms and hands to his body. He was lifted off his feet. There was Paul's voice in his ear. "You didn't oughta take any notice of what a guy like me says, Mr. Reed. I'm what they call a pathological liar." A moment later, he was slammed face forward into the wall with all Paul's weight and strength behind him. The lights went out all over the world.

EIGHT

The fire was bright and warm and it crackled cheerfully. It reminded him of November fifth, when most kids in England let off fireworks and burn effigies of Guy Fawkes on huge bonfires in all the parks and back yards.

No, it didn't, it reminded him of Christmas, when he was a kid and there was always a big fire burning in the sitting room, and Santa Claus had just dropped down the chimney and was bending over him asking him dumb questions.

"Are you all right, son?" Fogerty asked again.

James struggled to a sitting position. It hurt like hell. He was on the grass, on the far side of the swimming pool. Twenty-five yards away, the house was well alight, flames licking from the downstairs windows, already establishing a foothold on the second floor. In the distance, he heard the sound of the approaching fire trucks.

"I ain't askin' again, son. Are you all right?"

"I don't know," said James. He started to struggle to his feet. Fogerty gave him a hand. Nothing appeared to be broken. Painfully twisted perhaps, but basically still sound.

"Yep!" said Fogerty. "I reckon you're okay."

"What happened?"

"I told you. I don't sleep much. So, I was up and about and I saw the flames. I called the fire department and came over to drag you out."

"How'd you know I was in there?"

"I saw you earlier when you smashed that window and climbed in." He shook his head. "Pretty sloppy work, son."

"What happened to the other man?"

"He took off fifteen, twenty minutes before I spotted the fire." He looked up towards the house as a crash announced that the floor between first and second had collapsed. At the same time, the fire department arrived and took over.

"Mind if I make a telephone call?" asked James.

Fogerty led him through a gap in the hedge, across his own front lawn and into the house. Mrs. Fogerty, a frail looking woman in her seventies, was clutching a small long-haired dachshund to her skinny bosom, leaning over the bannisters and looking worried.

"Go back to bed, Ada," said Fogerty.

"Are you sure?"

"Goddamn it, woman, do like I say. I'll be up soon as I take care of this young feller."

She looked towards James, wondering if she should smile or not. She decided against it and went back upstairs.

"You wanna drink?" Fogerty asked.

"Scotch?"

"You've got it. Phone's in there." He pointed towards a pair of double doors leading from the hall. "You want to make your call before or after talking to the police?"

"What police?"

"The police who'll be wanting to talk with you when I tell 'em how I found you trussed up like a turkey in a house that you had no business being in in the first place."

"Trussed?"

"Strapped. Hand behind your back. Feet together."

So, the straps he'd bought had come in useful after all. "Where'd you find me Mr. Fogerty?"

"Right there in the hall. I figured the fire must have started in the kitchen, so you had around five minutes after it took hold before you'd have been done to crisp. And if you don't figure to tell the local police 'bout all that, young feller, along with what you told me about the drug dealing what's been going on over there you, and me have got a problem."

"You're absolutely right, Mr. Fogerty," said James. "Just as soon as I make my phone call, we'll talk to them together."

Fogerty looked at him long and hard. "That's more like it. What do you want with your Scotch?"

"Another," said James.

Fogerty chuckled and started out to go fetch the booze.

"Mr. Fogerty" said James, "Thanks for dragging me out of there."

"You're welcome, son. Most fun I've had all summer."

Okay, the phone call was going to have to wait. But not too long. Right now, he had to get out of there before he was confronted by the Spring Lake police force. Not that he didn't trust them. They were probably extremely efficient at whatever it was they were required to do in Spring Lake. But the time they'd take sorting out the story James would have to tell them, didn't bear thinking about. He could wind up spending the rest of the summer and half the fall in Spring Lake.

As he came into the hall, he could hear Fogerty crashing around in the kitchen, collecting ice and glasses. He made for the front door and slipped out. As he headed up the driveway to the front gate, the roof of the McCoy house collapsed inwards, sending up an eruption of flaming sparks, enough to give every firefly in Spring Lake an inferiority complex for life. He didn't even stop to rubberneck at the McCoy front gate with the neighbors who had gathered in their nightgowns and pajamas. He went straight to the nearest pay phone. That's when he discovered that his billfold was missing. Cash, credit cards, ID, everything gone. All Paul had left him was seventy-five cents in change. He placed a collect call to Mustapha Zee in New York. Mustapha refused to accept the call. James hung up and tried again through a different operator. This time he got lucky.

"Man, this is gonna cost you!" said Mustapha.

James told him what he wanted and Mustapha told him exactly how much it was going to cost. Webber's second five grand was disappearing fast, but he was in no position to argue.

"Where shall I get in touch?" Mustapha asked.

James told him to call him at the hotel.

Mustapha chuckled, "I just thought of something, man. He stole your money, right?"

"Right."

"So how you gonna get back to New York?"

"Any ideas?"

"Call a cab" said Mustapha.

It was four in the morning. He walked to the train station. The station was closed. The first train bound for New York was due at seven thirty. Three and a half hours to wait. For a short time, he gave serious thought to stealing a car. Then reason prevailed. He found a convenient bench and stretched out. Perhaps he could snatch a couple of hours sleep before starting on another day which, if he was any judge, was going to be a real bitch.

But the bench wasn't comfortable. Added to which, from where he was sitting, he could still see the glow in the night sky that marked the dying remains of the McCoy house. He was supposed to be feeding those flames himself. Some judge of character he'd turned out to be. Nice, simple, good natured Paul Menzies was a pyromaniacal psychopath. A homicidal fire raiser. A people torcher. The only surprise was that he hadn't set fire to the Beverly Hillcrest hotel after he'd done in Megan McCoy. Or to Megan herself for that matter. Wrong! That wasn't the only surprise. An even bigger one was the fact that James realized he had been suckered in all the way, not once, but twice. Whether that meant Paul Menzies was smart or James Reed was stupid, he didn't want to think about. But next time he was going to take no chances, assuming that there was going to be a next time.

The sun came up around five thirty. Now it was a static pall of grey smoke that marked where the fire had been, waiting for a sea breeze to disperse it. But it wasn't too pronounced, not enough to mar what was obviously going to be another sparking Spring Lake day. The fire department had obviously done their job. James wondered if Fogerty had done his job and informed the local police yet that there was a man from Scotland Yard chasing drug dealers all over their jurisdiction, hoping to make a bust and getting himself near killed in the process. Now that it was daylight, James decided he couldn't stay where he was on the bench. A prowling police car would pick him up for sure. Spring Lake was the kind of place where vagrants were escorted to the city limits and warned not to return or they'd likely be shot. There was no chance of finding a coffee shop open for another hour or two at least and he only had seventy-five cents anyway. So what the hell to do? He wound up doing nothing.

He walked around the park once, staying clear of the McCoy house. He strolled along the boardwalk and watched a couple of dawn fishermen standing waist deep in the Atlantic catching nothing but colds. At seven fifteen, he was back at the station.

Fortunately, he needed to take a pee. That's how he saw the bank of lockers, tucked away in a rarely used corner of the station. Even before he examined them, he knew he'd find Number 39 was in use. Trouble was, the key was in New York. He could try forcing the lock or he could come back later with the key or he could mail the key to Webber and tell him where to find the locker. But he was curious. A lot had gone down these past few days over what was in that locker. A couple of people had been killed, a couple more beat up, and somebody had tried to burn him alive. He figured he was entitled. He walked back out to the parking lot and located a car with the trunk unlocked. He took a screwdriver from the tool kit and used it to force the locker. The only guy on duty at the station was in his office making coffee, so he was undisturbed. Inside the locker was a manila envelope containing half a dozen 8 x 10 black and white prints of a naked man chewing on Paul Menzies cock. Paul was plainly identifiable. He was grinning into camera. The other guy was half hidden behind Paul and he was leaning forward concentrating on what he was doing. His face could hardly be seen. This, coupled with the terrible quality of the photographs made him unidentifiable. It could have been Jackson Webber, but it could have been almost anyone else, too. As blackmail material, it was hardly worth the paper it was printed on. The negatives were paper clipped to one of the prints. James banged on the door to the ticket office and asked to borrow some matches. He burned everything in the parking lot, replaced the screwdriver he'd borrowed, and went back to wait the arrival of the New York train. It arrived on time and he was one of a dozen people to board. When the guard came through checking tickets, he made a great show of just discovering that his billfold was missing. He gave the guard a fictitious name and address, promising to forward his fare as soon as possible.

He arrived at Penn Station an hour later, tired and hungry. He had a cab drive him to the Gramercy Park Hotel. There he collected the money Webber had given him. He paid the cab then he called and reported his credit cards missing. He told the guy at the desk that he was expecting a very important telephone call and he'd be in the restaurant having breakfast. Without even going upstairs, he went into the restaurant and ordered himself the largest breakfast he could. He'd managed to get through half a cup of coffee before he was called to the phone. It was Mustapha.

"How you doin', man."

"I'll tell you when you tell me how you're doin'."

"Just like you said pappy. Soon as you hung up, I high tailed it round to the apartment block on Fifth and prepared for a long sit. Only I don't have to wait hardly no time. Out she comes, into that little bitty car of hers and takes off like Al Unser. I follow her across the river to Jersey City where she goes to the bus station. There she hangs around 'til she picks up this guy who arrives on a bus."

"What did he look like?"

"Big motherfucker."

That described Paul adequately enough. "Where did they go?"

"Right back here, man."

"Fifth Avenue?"

"You got it."

"Hang around 'til I get there," said James.

"How long, man?"

"The money I'm paying you, what do you care?"

James didn't think Patsy or Paul would be going anywhere, so he finished his breakfast before walking the ten blocks. Mustapha was parked across the street from the apartment building arguing with an attractive young black woman who wanted him to drive her uptown to Bloomingdales. He pointed to James as the reason he couldn't oblige and she flounced off.

"See what you cost me, man," he said to James. "Her and me could have made sweet, sweet music,"

James wasn't in the mood for small talk. "They still there?"

"All I can tell you is they ain't come out the front entrance and her car is still parked down the side street."

"What are the chances of getting hold of another gun?"

"You gotta be kiddin' me!"

"Can you or can't you?" said James.

"Man, your attitude is real shitty this morning. What happened out there in the boonies, anyway? Where's the shooter you already go?"

"I don't have it any longer."

"The guy with the muscles take it off you? Some tough guy you're turning out to be."

"Don't give me a hard time," said James.

"I ain't giving you nothing, man. And right now I'm getting real pissed off with you. So how about you payin' the money you owe me. That way we'll be quits and I can forget I ever saw your honky face."

"What about a gun?"

"You ain't safe to have a gun man." He held out his hand. "The money motherfucker."

"When I'm good and ready," said James.

"The way you deal with the bad guys you're gonna be dead and buried before you're good and ready." He shook his head. "Shit man, what am I gonna do with you?"

James thought about it for a few seconds. "How about making a delivery for me?"

He sent Mustapha to find a flower shop while he looked for a sporting goods store. They met up again fifteen minutes later. Mustapha with an opulent looking bouquet of flowers, James with a baseball bat still in its presentation box. They crossed the street together. James hung back to check the sign outside giving the name of the company who managed the building. GROSS & GROSS. By the time he walked into the front hall, Mustapha was talking to the guy behind the desk.

"I got my job to do, man, n' ma job says I gotta get Ms. McCoy's personal signature for these flowers or it's my ass."

"I'll sign for them."

"You already said that 'n I already told you, I ……"

But the desk man wasn't even listening any longer. He was looking at James who was heading for the elevators. "Hey! Mister! Where do you think you're going?"

"Upstairs," said James.

"Not without I announce you first, you're not."

"Listen man, I gotta deliver these flowers," said Mustapha.

"Wait until I finish with this guy. Who do you wanna see?" he asked James again.

"If I don't get these delivered and collect me a signature, I'm gonna be out of a job and one dark night you're going to get yours up some dark alley," said Mustapha.

"Go deliver the fucking things," said the door man. "Apartment 1209." He turned back to James, "Now who do you wanna see, Mister?"

"We got a complaint," James said.

"Who's we?"

"I'm from Gross and Gross." These were the guys who paid his wages.

"Yes sir, what kind of complaint?"

"No big deal," said James. "The old lady on the the … I forget the floor, the one with the little dog."

"Mrs. Henshaw, eleven forty-three," said the door man with absolute certainty.

"That's the one," said James.

"What's her problem this time?"

"Listen, if I knew I'd have dealt with it over the phone. But she calls my boss and my boss calls me and tells me to get on down here and deal with it."

"If she tells you I kicked her dog, she's lying."

"I'll bear it in mind," said James. He turned towards the elevator that Mustapha had just gotten in, "Hold it a second."

Mustapha hit the hold button long enough for James to join him in the elevator. The doors slid shut and he pressed the button for the twelfth floor.

"You're something else, man," said Mustapha. "How'd you know there was an old woman with a dog?"

"There always is," said James.

They got out on the twelfth floor. James unwrapped the baseball bat from its box and walked with Mustapha to the door of 1209. He stood back as Mustapha rang the bell. Nothing happened for a long time. He rang the bell again. Finally, they heard Patsy on the other side of the door. Obviously, she had checked Mustapha out through the spyhole.

"What do you want?"

"Flowers for Ms. McCoy," said Mustapha

"Who from?"

"Shit lady, I just deliver them. Now you want'em or you don't?"

"Wait a minute."

There was the sound of bolts being slid back and a chain being unhooked. A moment later the door was open.

"You gotta sign for them," said Mustapha.

Patsy McCoy took a step out into the passage. She saw James immediately, but before she could say or do anything, Mustapha had dropped the flowers and grabbed her, wrapping none large hand over her mouth and lifting her off her feet. James ran into the apartment. The living room was empty. At the far side the door beyond stood open into the bedroom. James crossed the living room quickly and quietly. As he came into the bedroom, Paul Menzies was standing by the bed just dragging on his pants. James was taking no chances. Paul didn't even have time to register surprise at seeing James alive before he was doubled over from a whack across the kidney with the baseball bat, followed by another to the side of the head.

Paul measured his length on the bedroom floor and James hit him once more behind the ear to make sure. He was going through Paul's pants pockets when Mustapha came into the bedroom. He was still holding Patsy, one hand over her mouth, her feet clear of the floor.

"You can take your hand off her mouth," said James. "She's not going to yell now."

Mustapha removed his hand.

"You fucking bastards, what do you mean by busting into my fucking apart...."

Mustapha clapped his hand over her mouth again.

"I hate to hear a pretty lady use bad language," he said.

James had recovered his billfold from Paul's pants. He turned to Patsy, "Where's the gun?"

She tried to say something from behind Mustapha's hand. He removed his hand.

"Go fuck yourself," she said. "You, too, you black bastard."

"Hey man, we got us a racist," said Mustapha. "Don't get too many of them these days, it ain't fashionable."

"Pig," said Patsy.

"Come on lady, you can do better than that."

She spat in his eye. He hauled back a few inches and slapped her hard. "Maybe you and I should go next door for a couple of minutes while I teach you some manners," he said. Then he looked towards James, "What do you want I should do with her?"

"Soon as I find the gun you can split," said James. He nodded at the unconscious Paul. "Did he have a bag with him when she picked him up?"

"A carryall." Mustapha glanced around the bedroom. "That's it, over here."

James went to the corner of the room where a small canvas carryall had been dropped. He unzipped it and after groping around for a few seconds, came up with the gun. He checked it was still loaded. Then he came over to Patsy, who was still being held tight by Mustapha.

"I'll say this once," he said, "Your boyfriend there told me last night that I wasn't the kind of guy who'd use a gun. Maybe last night that was true. But that was before he tried to burn me alive. Last night is behind us, we're into a bright, new day and right now nothing in this world would give me greater pleasure than to use this gun on him, or you, if you give me any trouble. Understand?"

Obviously, she did because she didn't even cuss. She just nodded her head. James turned to Mustapha, "Okay, you can split."

"You want I should hang around outside?"

"I already told you what I want you to do," said James.

"Right man! You've got it. Y'all take care now." A moment later he was gone.

"Go sit on the bed," said James.

She and Paul had obviously been screwing when the doorbell had rung. She had pulled on a short terry robe, which now gaped at the front clear down to her navel. She made no attempt to cover up. Possibly she was unaware of the effect that her small, tight breasts had on James, but it was unlikely She glanced at Paul, still motionless, face down on the floor.

"Is he dead?" she asked.

"I have no idea," lied James. "It doesn't matter anyway, it's you I want to talk to."

"I had nothing to do with last night."

"Maybe not directly, but that's not what we're going to talk about. I want to know why you killed your stepmother."

She looked at him wide eyed. "You're crazy," she said.

"I assume that means you're not going to tell me."

Paul gave a small groan without moving. She glanced down at him then back to James. "Is he going to be alright?"

"Eventually," said James.

"He told me you wanted to send him to prison. He'll never go you know. He's told me that lots of times. Whatever happens he said, I'll never go to prison."

"He doesn't have to worry about that any more. I've withdrawn the option."

"What do you mean?"

"Prison is now no longer on his agenda."

"I don't understand."

"Later you will. On the other hand, you're something else. You could do twenty years."

"I didn't kill Megan."

"I didn't and Paul says he didn't and those crazy guys Webber hired didn't. I'm afraid you're the only one left."

"Why would I kill her?"

"Because she was screwing around with your boyfriend and because you wanted this." He pulled the locker key from his pocket and held it up.

"What's that?"

"It's the key to a locker, Megan gave it to me."

"You've had it right from the start! When I came to see you in Malibu."

James nodded.

She looked at him a long moment, then she shook her head slowly from side-to-side. "You're a cunning bastard, James Reed."

James didn't bother arguing with her.

Now she decided a change of tactics might be in order. She put her hands flat on the bed behind her and leaned back. The robe fell from one shoulder entirely. 'What do you care anyway, who killed Megan? You told me yourself she was nothing to you."

"Cover yourself up," said James.

She glanced down at her nakedness as though aware of it for the first time. Then back up to James. "Do I turn you on?"

There wasn't much point in lying. "Yes," said James.

"So let's fuck," she said. She stood up and slipped the robe off entirely. She was completely naked, her slim, pale body looking as though it belonged to a fifteen-year-old. The impression of extreme youth was heightened by the fact that she had shaved her pubic hair. "I'll do anything you like. We could tie Paul up and when he comes round we could make him watch." So much for fidelity thought James. "You could…maybe you could do something with that gun, I mean…something sexy." One of her hands started to stroke her breast, the other wandered down between her legs. The phone rang suddenly. Patsy looked at it, then at James.

"It's probably for me," said James. He transferred the gun to his other hand and picked up the phone.

"Hi, Reed," said Gary. "Is what the black guy told me kosher?"

"Absolutely," said James

"Be right over." The line went dead.

James put the phone down. "We're having company in a few minutes. You better put some clothes on."

She looked confused for a moment. "Company? The police?"

"No police. Just a bunch of guys who are really pissed off that one of their friends got burned to death by lover boy there."

She didn't get it at first. When she did, she started to look frightened. "They scare me, those men."

"At least you don't have to worry about rape."

"No, honestly, please listen." She tailed off.

"I'm listening," said James.

"If I tell you, then will you let me go?"

"You don't have to tell me, I already know."

"It wasn't as if I meant to kill her. I was really angry. I mean, her trying to take Paul away from me. When you called for her, I followed you. Then when you dropped her back at the hotel, I went up to her room. We had a terrible argument. She called me all kinds of names and said she and Paul had been lovers since forever and I was a joke and not fit to lick his boots. I told her a couple of the things Paul had said about her being an old lady who he was doing a big favor by screwing and she got violent. I pushed her or hit her, I don't remember. She fell down and didn't get up. It was an accident. Then I got frightened. I didn't know what to do, I just turned and ran."

"That's a good story, except she was strangled to death with her tights. Explain to me how that was an accident. Take your time thinking about it."

At that moment, Paul decided to join the proceedings. He groaned a couple of times and rolled over onto his back. His eyes remained shut for a long time, then they opened and focused on Patsy who was standing practically over him.

"Hey girl." Then, "What …" Then he remembered. He turned his head until he saw James with the gun in one hand and the baseball bat in the other. He held a look for what seemed a long time then shook his head. "You're something else, Mr. Reed, you surely to God are something else." He started to get to his feet.

"Stay where you are," said James. Paul conscious was Paul dangerous.

"What if I don't?"

"I'll break your legs," said James.

Paul looked at him steadily, searching perhaps for a sign of hesitation or reluctance. Obviously, he couldn't find one. He relaxed back on the floor.

"Put some clothes on," Paul said to Patsy, without even looking at her.

"Mind your own business," she said.

He turned and looked at her, then across at James. Then he laughed, "If you think screwing him is going to get you off the hook, you're even dumber than I thought."

"Shut up."

"Dumb bimbo."

She kicked him in the side. He grabbed her ankle and twisted it, bringing her down across him.

"Bastard," she said. She went for his face with her fingernails, but he held her off easily. She rolled away from him and he rolled over on top of her.

"Stupid cunt!" he said. He hauled back and slapped her hard. She went glassy-eyed. "Stupid, dumb, cunt. If it hadn't been for you, he'd never have found me." He slapped her again.

"That's enough," said James.

He didn't get through. Paul slapped Patsy once more, much harder this time. James moved close and pressed the gun hard into the back of Paul's neck. "Knock it off."

It seemed like there was a moment of hesitation, one fraction of time as Paul weighed the consequences. Then he hit Patsy again. This time he didn't slap her, he doubled up his fist and punched in the middle of her forehead. James dropped the gun and used the baseball bat two handed, bringing down across the back of Paul's neck. He collapsed, like a slaughtered ox, completely covering Patsy beneath him. James rolled him off and examined her briefly. Blood was coming from her ears. He'd guessed right. She was dead. The back of her head had been on the floor when Paul punched her. He might as well have dropped a ten-ton weight on her. And right at this moment, the phone rang. It was the front desk. "There's some men here say they've got an appointment."

"Send them up," said James.

He walked into the living room and poured himself a large scotch. Two minutes later, he opened the door to Gary and two of his guys.

"Where is he?" Gary asked.

James nodded towards the bedroom. Gary crutched his way to the bedroom door and looked in. He turned back to James.

"He's the guy who croaked Bill, right?"

James nodded.

"Is he dead?"

"No."

"Good. Who's the broad?"

"Patsy McCoy."

"He croak her too?"

James nodded. "Can you take care of it?"

"No problem. She can go with him when we're through. Anything you need?"

"Nope," said James.

"See you around," said Gary.

James came out of the apartment building. It was another scorcher of a day. New York in high summer was hell on earth. Mustapha was parked across the street talking to a black lady who was wheeling a couple of white kids in a stroller. James crossed over.

"Where you wanna go, man?" Mustapha asked.

"Home," said James.

"Gramercy Park Hotel, right?"

"Kennedy Airport," said James.

He couldn't wait to get home and he promised himself that he'd never come back. Nothing good ever happened to him in New York.

THE END

ABOUT THE AUTHOR
AND THIS BOOK

Jimmy Sangster, who died in 2011, was an acclaimed screen-writer (*Curse of Frankenstein, Deadlier Than the Male, The Legacy,* etc), director (*Lust for a Vampire, Banacek,* etc), TV writer (*Wonder Woman, Cannon, Movin' On, BJ and The Bear, The Magician, Kolchak: The Night Stalker,* etc) and novelist (*Touchfeather, Touchfeather Too, The Spy Killer* and *Foreign Exchange*).

He was also the author of three James Reed crime novels — *Snowball, Blackball* and *Hardball* – which were published in the late 1980s. The Reed books earned him critical praise, respectable sales, and a TV series option from a major studio. All of that was enough incentive to convince Sangster to write a fourth novel in the series. But, as he wrote in his 1997 autobiography *Do You Want It Good or Tuesday?*, he believed that the only way to get the publisher to invest the kind of marketing and promotion dollars into the series that he felt it deserved was to "get him to pay such a large advance that he'd simply have no choice. Either the book sells, or he loses his shirt. Maybe it would have worked for Elmore Leonard or Ed McBain, but not for Jimmy Sangster. They refused to increase my advance. My New York agent told them to take a jump, she'd sell it elsewhere."

She couldn't find another publisher willing to step up and that was the end of the James Reed series of books.

Or so it seemed.

Nearly twenty-five years later, we came along and licensed the rights from the Sangster estate to reprint all of his novels.

We'd already republished four of his spy novels, and were about to start work on the James Reed series, when we finally got around to reading his autobiography and learned, much to our surprise, that the manuscript for a fourth novel might exist somewhere. We immediately reached out to his estate and learned that the manuscript was among his papers, archived at the Cinema and Television History Institute at De Montfort University in Leicester, England.

We secured the rights from the Sangster estate to publish the book and our good friend Stephen Gallagher, the acclaimed UK-based novelist, screenwriter and television producer (and a big admirer of Jimmy Sangster) volunteered to visit the university and make us a copy of the manuscript – which turned out to be a faded, dot-matrix print-out covered with handwritten corrections and revisions. Stephen saved the manuscript to PDF and emailed it to us.

We read it and loved it. Our office manager Denise Fields retyped the manuscript, our co-founder Lee Goldberg edited it, and now we're honored and delighted to bring you the first, and probably last, new Jimmy Sangster novel in thirty years.